Foxy Mysteries Book 5

Dead

Cold

I0593741

1

Liz rubbed her arms to stimulate circulation in the cool, bright, artificially lit laboratory. A backlit table sat like an island in the middle of the white tiled room with bones of a long dead victim laid out on display. She couldn't help but wonder why the room was so frigid—surely bones didn't decompose?

The yellow stained skeleton was set out with every limb displayed in order and precisely as it would have been in life. Liz shuddered, unsure exactly how she felt about being drawn into this investigation.

Barely six months into her new career as a PI, Liz felt out of her depth dealing with a decade old death. But this case wasn't about her. It was about Jack and his past.

She watched from a distance, across the room and near the door. A sudden wave of claustrophobia forced her to take long, slow breaths as the forensic anthropologist pointed to a bone fragment.

The enlarged image displayed on an LCD screen as the electronic microscope hovered over the woman's skull. Looking at the bone through magnification, on the monitor, made it less real, less confronting. She watched Jack's emotions roll from determination to genuine grief, then on to anger and frustration.

She wondered why Jack had agreed to lead the investigation into the suspicious death of his former girlfriend— ten years after she'd gone missing. Liz could see from his expression and the stiffness of his posture that it was proving more difficult than he'd anticipated.

'The victim suffered a fractured skull. The force required to cause such an injury in this part of the cranium is extreme.' The forensic anthropologist was in her late fifties, tall and lean. She wore reading glasses that covered only the lower half of her eyes completing a stereotypical college professor look.

'You think it's the cause of death then?' Jack asked, not taking his eyes from the body.

'Cause of death is inconclusive, but the impact from this blow,' she put her finger on the upper left forehead of the skull, which featured a deep, narrow hole with fractures like spider webs fanning out around it, 'most certainly incapacitated the victim. Without toxicology, or human tissue, we have nothing else to use to determine exactly what killed this woman. However, there is no doubt in my mind that she met with foul play, that may not have been the cause of death, but ultimately led to her demise.'

'Thanks.' Jack's tone lacked any conviction. Liz watched as he hovered over the remains a moment, before turning to leave. Seeing Liz and her PI business partner standing back beside him almost startled him, so deep was he in his own world of pain. He recovered quickly. 'Liz, Max. Any questions?'

Liz looked at Max and waited. He was the former detective and Jack's ex-partner. As much as she didn't want to admit it, she knew nothing about forensics or murder scenes. She wondered again why Jack had even wanted her here, in the cold caverns of the basement, the silence of death all around her.

'I think we have everything we can get here mate. Let's regroup over some lunch. And a beer.' Max grinned, but Jack didn't return the gesture.

'You might want these?' The anthropologist held up a large zip-lock plastic bag containing a pair of gold stud earrings, a bracelet watch and a gold signet ring. Jack shook his head. The bag seemed excessive for the meagre remnants of the woman's personal effects.

'Keep it with all the evidence for now.'

'If you're sure.' The doctor moved back to the remains, placing the bag on a stainless-steel tray alongside the skull.

Liz followed both men from the room, into a corridor that led past an autopsy suite. She averted her eyes, not wanting to accidentally glimpse blood or tissue today. Since becoming a PI and leaving her escort work behind, she'd seen death, including her best friend's body, but this case felt different and her stomach was turning even more than her mind.

When Max first told her that Jack had a case he wanted them to consult on, she was surprised. Even more so when Max failed to explain Jack's former girlfriend was the victim. She knew Marilyn had left Jack, without any explanation ten years before, but he'd never talked about the details.

Now they were going to have to drag up the past and find out why she was dead, how long she'd been so and whether she was a victim of a mugging, or something more sinister. At least this time around, Jack would be able to pull phone and banking records to help, but the fact that Jack was even on the case at all, disturbed Liz. Not that she thought he'd actually have hurt Marilyn, but since partners were nearly always the first suspect, it felt wrong to Liz to have him leading the team.

So far, she'd kept the opinion to herself. Maybe calling Max in to consult on the investigation was Jack's way of making sure everything he did stayed above board in his boss' eyes, but Liz knew the Chief, intimately, they had history from her escort days, but something about the way Jack had been handed the case made her feel apprehensive.

'Not sure about the beer Max, but we should go over the case files and see where we want to get started.' Jack held the door and waved Max and Liz through. They took the elevator to the ground floor and embraced the early spring sun which greeted them. Liz felt the warmth penetrate her core and resisted the urge to rotate in the warm glow. The feelings of unease about the case drifted away with the white puffy clouds that floated over the lush green parklands of Victoria Square.

2

Liz sat down at her favourite table, the chequered tablecloth fluttering in the light spring air. Nino came out to the front of the restaurant with menus and a jug of chilled water. The elm trees had sprung to life with new green growth sprouting from the old, hard winter pruning.

Max took the menu from Nino and handed one to Jack who put it down on the table, disinterested.

'I'll have a cappuccino Nino, a latte for Jack.' She took the liberty of ordering because she knew the detective well enough now to read his moods. When he was stewing on something, food didn't interest him.

'I'll have a Coopers Pale Ale thanks Nino.'

The waiter smiled. 'How's Jackie doing?'

Liz should have realised Nino would mention her daughter. The last time he'd seen Jack, he'd been racing out the door to meet Jackie after Liz had been kidnapped. 'She's good Nino. I'll bring her in for dinner soon. Sorry we missed the last reservation.'

'I'm just happy you're both okay. Let me know when you're ready to order.' He moved inside to get the drinks, well accustomed to the small band of detectives working together to solve crimes in his quaint, authentic, Italian restaurant across the road from the bustling Adelaide Railway Station.

'You know his accent disappeared when I took off after you last month. Aussie as they come.' Jack seemed to perk up as he thought about the restaurant owner.

'His father's accent is thick as, but Nino has lived here all his life. It doesn't surprise me.' Liz didn't waste time. Jack was pulling himself out of his stupor and keeping him out of the doldrums was more important than how she felt about working on a case involving Jack's ex. 'So who was Marilyn working with when she went missing?'

Jack didn't need to refer to the files. 'She was an accountant for *Guild and Glover*.'

'Qualified or a bookkeeper?'

'Does it make a difference?' Max scrunched his nose, wondering why she'd asked.

'It can. Accountants tend to sign off on the work bookkeepers do. They don't get to dig around with all the figures too much.'

'She was an accountant, but not certified with the APA yet. She needed to work fulltime for a certified accountant to apply to be accredited.'

Nino arrived with the drinks. 'Ready to order yet?'

'Sorry Nino, give us a minute, we got carried away chatting. We'll be ready shortly.' Liz already knew what she wanted, but Jack was yet to pick up his menu.

'It's fine. I never got to finish that lasagne last time Nino, so I'll have that again,' Jack offered, looking to Max to see if he was ready to order.

'I'll have the Osso Bucco mate.' Nino nodded his approval and looked toward Liz.

'I think Veal Scaloppini will be ideal today thanks Nino. I won't have to cook dinner tonight that way.'

'Done. Won't be long.'

'Alright. That's probably where we can start.' Liz was straight back to business. 'We need to speak to her employer and find out what accounts she was working on at the time.'

'I've already requested her phone records from the telecommunications company, and her banking records. Jenny has been running through the phone calls. I wish I'd dug deeper back in '09. Maybe I could have found Marilyn before someone killed her.'

'It's not just on you mate. None of us thought anything bad had happened.' Max patted Jack's shoulder firmly.

'Do we know how long she's been dead?' Liz hadn't heard the anthropologist mention it.

'Not yet, they need to run some carbon dating scans but will need to fully examine and x-ray the bones first.' Liz was surprised at Max's confident explanation at first, but considering he'd been a detective for ten years, she should have expected he'd understand how the pathology worked.

'Did she give you any indication that someone was bothering her?' Liz spun her cup around so the handle was on the right side.

'She'd been preoccupied but it was tax prep time and she was knee-deep in paperwork. I hadn't seen any indication there was anything bothering her.'

'No old boyfriends that we need to chase up?'

'We got together in our early thirties, so there are bound to be some ex's but we never talked about them. No one serious that I knew of.' Jack hadn't touched his coffee.

'Drink your coffee. You need the caffeine to kick you into gear,' Liz suggested as she took another sip of her own drink.

'I don't think there's any hurry. She's probably been dead for nearly ten years, so most of the evidence is likely going to take some serious digging to find.' Jack seemed to deflate as the concept sank in.

'Not necessarily. Marilyn's body coming to light is going to make someone very uncomfortable. If they left any evidence behind, they'll be pulling out all stops to hide it now.' Max drained half his beer in one long swig.

'Hey. I hope you're not blowing your health kick now that Jackie's graduation is over.' Liz waved a finger at her business partner. Their life was complicated now, yet with a business partnership, the lines were clearly drawn, not like their past together. A short, tumultuous marriage had been bad for both of them, but their daughter Jackie had been the one good thing to come out of their relationship.

'I really enjoyed getting into shape to show her snobby adoptive mother I wasn't a useless ex-cop, but no, I'm not blowing it now. I was just thirsty.' He grinned and Liz was glad to see Jack shake his head good-naturedly.

'We need to confirm Marilyn had never filed for a restraining order against any ex-boyfriend or family members. We need to interview work mates and her employer to find out if they knew what she was working on and who she was socializing with when she wasn't with me back then. We can interview her clients too if necessary. Anything else?' Jack summarized.

Nino arrived with a plate in each hand and another balanced carefully on his forearm. He placed the meals in front of everyone, nodded, smiled politely and turned to give them privacy without a word.

'So Liz and I can't interview the work associates, that's outside our jurisdiction, what do you want us to do?' Max picked up his cutlery, not bothering to wait for anyone else to get started.

'I'll get Jenny to pass Marilyn's bank statements over to you along with her phone records. Maybe one of you can find something there?' Max sighed with the idea of paperwork.

'What about any personal effects?' Liz knew Jack wouldn't have thrown anything out. He was a little OCD, so they would all be filed away neatly and likely catalogued, but Marilyn's life with Jack had to be documented somewhere.

'Marilyn had no family in Adelaide, so I kept what she left behind, which wasn't much. Her clothing I donated to charity.'

'Nothing was taken, no clothing, a suitcase?' Jack didn't answer. 'And you really didn't think anything terrible had happened to her?' For the first-time Liz was wondering if Jack really was as innocent as he appeared.

'I reported her missing. I took a month off work trying to track her last movements. But without any proof anything had happened to her, we couldn't get a warrant to trace her phone or bank records. Any judge I asked, and I asked them all, said she could have been running from a prior life and didn't want to be found. They couldn't invade her privacy.'

Liz could see the anguish and hear the sense of hopelessness in Jack's voice. His obsessive personality must have caused him no end of anxiety over the disappearance and maybe he'd never truly put it behind him.

'I'll go over her things. If you don't mind?' Liz patted his hand as Max shovelled a large fork load of succulent meat into his cavernous mouth.

'I'll drop them by your house tonight.'

3

Jenny stood next to Jack, waiting patiently for him to process the scene. He knew she was giving him time to get his act together emotionally, but he was confused about his own feelings. On the one hand, he really wanted to find out what happened to Marilyn, but on the other, he was worried his past relationship might put a wedge between him and Liz.

'Her bones were found here.' Jack lifted the police tape and Jenny followed him beyond the line into the turned earth of a construction site at the back of Adelaide Oval. 'They moved the utility shed about a month ago and broke ground on the stadium extension three weeks ago.'

'Who found the first bones?' Jenny squatted down and examined the well-turned soil.

'An excavator driver noticed the discoloured femur first. He didn't realise it was human until another construction worker on site started waving his hands around. When he stopped, he got out and saw the skull.'

'Did forensics find anything useful on scene?'

'Nothing they've reported yet.'

'Can we find out when the concrete was poured on the utility shed?'

'That's your next job after we interview the staff at *Guild and Glover*.'

'How are you going with all this?' Jenny's stare was intense and Jack looked away. He'd worked with the new detective when Max had retired less than six months ago, but he'd known her nearly two years since she was promoted to detective. She had a sharp mind, didn't miss much at all. If she was asking how he was going, he was wearing his emotions on his sleeve, something a lead detective on a suspected homicide couldn't afford to do.

'Frustrated, but we'll move forward quickly now we can get the information we need. Let's get to *Guild and Glover*.'

****

The foyer was tiled in sparkling charcoal high gloss porcelain, bordered by smoked glass offices framed with modern plush tweed sofas featuring polished stainless-steel legs. Jack adjusted his suit jacket, did up the front button and reached for his badge trying not to feel like he'd stepped back into his past life.

A Pultney Grammar boy, with a Magistrate Judge and Doctor for parents, he'd lived this life before becoming a cop. He'd hated it then, he hated it even more now. Not once had he attended any of Marilyn's work parties, something that hadn't bothered her, but now it bothered him.

If he'd paid more attention, maybe Marilyn would still be alive. Their relationship had never been based on chemistry, but he'd cared deeply for her and they'd been good for each other.

'I'm Senior Detective Cunningham, this is Detective Williams.' He wasn't sure why he'd thrown the Senior in, but he suspected it was the opulent surroundings that made him feel the need to put more clout behind his enquiry.

'What can we do for you Detectives?' The receptionist wore neutral makeup, her hair was tied up in a loose bun—her suit costing more than Jack's car—which wasn't saying much since his old BMW had been with him since he left high-school.

'I'd like to speak to your HR Department about a former employee.'

'Take a seat. I'll have someone come down as soon as possible.' Jack put his badge back in his jacket pocket and drummed his fingers on the counter, ignoring the request to find a comfortable chair.

The receptionist watched him as she clicked buttons on her phone system and adjusted her mic. 'Detectives to see you Claude, about an HR matter.' She looked pained as she waited for an answer. 'No, they don't have an appointment.'

Jenny paced in front of the counter and Jack took a deep breath. 'I *can* come back with a warrant.' He spoke loud enough to ensure that not only Claude *whoever Claude was* could hear, but also so two or three people waiting outside various offices in the large foyer.

'Yes Sir. I'll tell them.' The receptionist pressed a button on her phone and held up her finger as she took another call. '*Guild and Glover*, Stephanie speaking, how can we help you?'

Jack moved away two steps, crossed his arms and waited for her to do her job. There was no point losing his cool with her. If HR didn't come down to speak with him, he'd get the warrant and then turn the place upside down. The thought gave him a weird sense of satisfaction, enough to know this case was getting to him more than he wanted it to.

'Mr Gregory will be with you shortly.' The receptionist spoke to Jack before taking another call.

He moved further away, satisfied for the moment. Leaning against a tiled pillar, he touched the leaves of a tall rubber plant, unsure if it was real or fake, and waited.

'An appointment?' Jenny scoffed. 'What is this place?'

'It's a top-shelf accounting firm. I knew Marilyn was pretty wrapped when she got the job here. The place is known for great pay and good working conditions but it also does the books for some of Adelaide's biggest firms.'

'That could mean they also do the books for some of Adelaide's undesirables.'

'Exactly what I was wondering, but I don't think a warrant will extend to the entire client list, just those that Marilyn worked on.'

'That's a pity. Hemi would love it if we uncovered something his federal task force could get stuck into.'

Jack thought about Hemi Anderson. The federal agent had proved himself invaluable in two of their recent cases. In the last, he'd been responsible for bringing Liz out of a deadly hostage situation alive. For that alone, Jack felt he owed the big Maori.

'If we find anything of use, I'll be sure Anderson gets wind of it.'

'He's always up for a challenge,' Jenny grinned.

'We know. He's dating you.' Jack returned the gesture.

'Detectives.' An older man in a charcoal suit that matched the tiles perfectly, moved forward. His ash-blonde hair was cut short and styled, his fake tan a little too orange and his teeth shone so brightly with whitener, Jack wished he'd worn his sunglasses.

'Mr Gregory, I assume?' Jack took the offered hand reluctantly but used a more forceful grip than he'd usually employ. There was something about the guy that just made it seem necessary. Maybe it was his George Michael five o'clock shadow or the fake grin that matched his fake tan—either way, Jack could see getting what he wanted from the guy, wasn't going to be easy.

4

Liz studied what was left of a dead woman's life and thought about her own legacy. Marilyn had gone missing and other than Jack, no one had really cared—no family, no friends, no one.

The image of Liz's mother popped into her head—short, curvy and artificially blonde with a tan that belied her English heritage—her mother had never liked living alone after her father died.

Thirty years had gone by quickly and she'd had nothing to do with the woman in all that time. She had her reasons, but were they strong enough to abandon someone and not care about them in any way?

Running away from abuse at the hands of her mother's boyfriend had landed her on the streets of Adelaide, selling herself to make ends meet. But that was behind her now, so the question running through her mind niggled at her. *Was it time to forgive her mother?*

She shook her head to physically eject the idea from her mind. Forcing herself to focus, she began opening one of the two plastic boxes that now contained what was left of Marilyn De Beer's life.

Jack had given away all the clothing, but these two boxes represented all that was left of a bright, talented woman.

The first box contained photo albums, and a box of letters which caught Liz's eye. She put them on the long white kitchen island bench to inspect later. As she flicked through the photos, she found the first album mostly filled with photos of Marilyn and Jack. They looked like a happy couple, nothing strange caught her eye.

The remaining three albums contained photos from events including birthday parties, Marilyn as a bridesmaid at a wedding, a group photo at a Christmas party. Moving on to the final album, she stopped.

A majestic landscape, full of tall trees and open plains made her breath catch. If the Baobab trees hadn't given away the location, the tall necked giraffe would have. The next photo was of Marilyn, in her mid-teens, with a group of African locals, their bright white smiles making Marilyn's death even sadder.

Liz pulled the photo from behind the clear cellophane cover and inspected the back for a description. There was nothing, so she replaced the photo and opened her laptop ready to make some notes.

She started with dot points – *Marilyn's South African history.* She finished with the box and returned to the albums before opening the second plastic container.

It contained souvenirs, a few accounting curriculum books, a postcard from South Africa and a handful of brochures from various jewellers around Adelaide. At the bottom of the box were four photos cut from magazines, featuring various designs of diamond rings. Liz wondered if Marilyn had been prompting Jack to propose before she went missing.

Thinking about Jack proposing invoked a long sigh. There was never going to be a diamond ring on her finger, even though she'd completely given up seeing clients after her last long-term client's murder. When Ted was killed, it had triggered Liz into rethinking her part-time occupation. She hadn't let the escort agency go, but she had handed all her clients on to younger girls.

Gifts had rolled in with emails begging her to keep on working and she'd politely replied thanking them for their generosity, but emphatically refusing to return to work. The sound of her door buzzer snapped her out of her daydream.

Moving to the tablet on her counter, Liz checked her security camera. Max's face loomed in the fish eye lens. She moved to the door and opened it. 'About time you got here.' Her tone was light.

'Coffee on?' Max moved to the kitchen counter and pulled out a stool. 'What's with this mess?' He surveyed the area, his eyes resting on the as yet unopened box of letters which stood out on the otherwise empty counter.

'It can be. You eaten?' Liz moved to her Miele coffee machine to select a cappuccino for Max, she pressed the button to begin the cycle.

'Yep. I'm good.' He patted his belly. 'Grabbed a bacon and egg muffin from Maccas on the way.'

'That's the Max I know,' she teased. He'd lost at least ten kilos recently, his shirt buttons no longer stretching over an expanding midriff, but take-away didn't fit his new commitment to staying healthy.

'I've got gym tonight. I can spare a few calories for a little junk food now and then.' He sounded defensive and Liz grinned.

'Alright tiger. No need to bite.' She handed him his coffee and moved to the fridge to replace the milk dispenser and get out the lactose-free milk to make her own coffee.

'Jenny said she's sending through the phone records and the banking details, in particular the credit cards for the month leading up to and just after Marilyn's disappearance.'

'That's good. Is she emailing me?' Liz moved to her computer and opened a browser tab, milk dispenser still in hand as she scrolled the mouse over her inbox. Ignoring the emails from *Foxy Escorts*, she opened *Fox Investigations* email account and waited for it to update.

'As far as I know. Yes.' Max took a sip of his coffee and sighed audibly. 'Great coffee.'

16

'Thanks.' Liz scrolled over an email from Jenny, tapping it open, the SA Police privacy warning reminding her she was dealing with sensitive information. 'Hey. What do you make of the Chief letting Jack lead this investigation?' She moved to make her own coffee.

Max shrugged. 'Jack's a good cop, besides, do you really think he'd let Bridges lead this one?'

Liz nodded. 'Yep, Jenny still doesn't really trust the guy. Ex Sydney-side cop, shipped off to Adelaide. He has to have upset someone.'

'Exactly. Besides. The Chief wants to keep Jack around and isn't an idiot. If he'd taken this case away from Jack, Jack would have gone on leave to pursue it anyway, or worse, he might have quit.'

'I hadn't thought of that.' Liz joined Max at the long countertop, coffee in hand. 'Jack dropped off Marilyn's personal effects.' She indicated the mess on the floor. 'I've been through everything. Do you know if she kept her own place at all? I haven't asked Jack.'

'You should talk to him about it. He brought you in on this case because he wants you to know about his past. You've shared yours with him when Gemma went missing, now it's his turn.'

'Yes, but I had to, he doesn't have to tell me about his life with Marilyn.'

'He does if he wants to find out why she died and who put that hole in her head.' Max reached for the box of letters he'd been eying off as they spoke. 'What are these?'

'I was afraid to look.'

'Why?' Max pulled the lilac coloured box over and studied it. The pattern on the outside looked personal, even romantic with lace and flower motifs all over it. Liz had left it until last, afraid it might have contained love letters, history about Jack and Marilyn's love life. She wasn't sure she was ready to read that.

'I don't know. It just looked, private, personal.'

Max's face showed his surprise. 'Not like you to stay out of someone else's business.'

'This is different. This is *Jack's* personal life. Those letters could be intimate.'

Max grinned mischievously. 'All the more reason to read them then.' He opened the lid to reveal at least twenty letters. He retrieved one and checked the postage stamp and date. 'South Africa, back when they used to postmark and date letters.'

'Back when they used letters full-stop you mean.' Liz took another sip of coffee, relieved they weren't from Jack. Max passed one to her for inspection. The letter was addressed to a different place from where Marilyn lived with Jack. She pulled her laptop over and added the address to her dot-point list.

'You want me to check it out?' Max peered over her shoulder as she typed.

'Maybe, but these letters are dated twenty years ago. How long had she been in Australia?'

Max shrugged. 'Jack met her when they were in their early thirties, maybe she came here for university?'

'I don't know. The timeline doesn't fit if she was only just getting fully qualified as an accountant when she went missing.'

'Maybe she finished uni here, went back to South Africa and came back later to do her accounting degree? Or maybe she finished her course and decided to try something different?' Max retrieved another letter from the box, the handwriting and address were the same.

'That looks like a female's handwriting.' Liz opened the letter and began to read. 'Looks like a pen pal or friend from the home she left behind.'

'Worth following up if we can find her.' Max turned the letter over and pointed to the return address. 'Botswana, Taiwo Moremi from Botswana Africa.'

'We'll start with Taiwo then. Maybe she spoke with Marilyn leading up to her death?'

5

'I think I'd rather have a colonoscopy than work with that guy.' Jenny opened the passenger's side-door and flopped down heavily into the old worn leather seat. 'Weren't you getting a new car when you made senior?'

'I was, but I've been rather busy. Framed by my secret half-sister while investigating my dad's poisoning, then trying to track down who killed Liz's client.'

'Liz managed to buy Max a new car over the phone during the investigation of a missing girl.' Jenny's expression was smug and Jack shook his head as he started the car.

'Well, Liz is the ultimate time manager. She does run an escort agency, take on clients of her own and actively run a PI firm after all.'

'No clients anymore.' Jenny smiled at Jack's surprise.

'None of my business.' The car pulled away from the curb of the swanky building and out into the line of traffic heading down King William Road from North Adelaide.' Jenny went to disagree, but Jack wasn't leaving the comment open for further discussion. '*Guild and Glover* operated out of a smaller office building in Glenelg when Marilyn worked for them in '09. Find out when they moved to North Adelaide.'

Jenny nodded, got her phone out and made some notes to follow up on later. 'Well if you aren't getting a new car, at least get a new phone. That old flip thing must have seen better days. Does it even have 4G on it?'

'It does. I thought it was retro, even trendy to have old tech.' Jenny rolled her eyes. 'You know I'm not keen on technology. I'll stick with this one for now.'

They pulled into the underground parking at the Angas Street Office and made their way to the elevator.

'Are you bringing Bridges in on this case?' Jenny pressed the call button and the doors opened a few seconds later.

'Not yet. He's helping out with that fraud investigation.'

'Oh, that guy is scum. Pretending to care about disabled women and conning them into giving him money. He's a real piece of work.'

'It's a tricky case.' Jack pressed third floor and the doors closed on the elevator. 'Some of the women he spent time with won't offer witness statements. They think he hasn't done anything wrong.'

'Yeah, but that one woman gave him her life savings when he told her he needed money for his sick mother, who'd been dead for five years.'

'No shortage of unscrupulous people in the world Williams.' The elevator doors opened and the detectives made their way down the short corridor to the Major Crimes office.

Bridges looked up from his desk across the room. 'How did you get past the press?'

'What press?' Jenny moved to her desk, opened the drawer and placed her handbag and gun inside.

'There have to be thirty reporters and cameras out front. How could you miss them?'

'We came in through the parking lot.' Jack put his own weapon in the drawer of his desk and placed his light-grey jacket over the back of his worn vinyl chair.

'Still, surprised they didn't swamp you at the entrance to the parking lot. The Chief has been fuming all morning. Seems the story about your ex broke this morning.'

'Well I didn't leak it. He knows how much I hate attention.'

'Well whoever told them had details, lots of them.'

'Shit. That means whoever attacked Marilyn is going to be getting out of town or covering their tracks even faster than we hoped.' Jenny moved her mouse to wake her computer back up, the screen slowly coming to life.

'Who knew about the case?' Jack sat down at his own computer and began hitting keys. 'Which paper broke the story?'

'Not a paper. That's why they are running around like loons trying to get a scoop.' Bridges looked pleased that he knew something Jack didn't, but his expression changed when he saw Jack's agitation. 'A Youtuber, based in Adelaide, covers unsolved murders.'

'Name!'

'She's a Youtuber. Her name might not be real.'

'Just tell him Bridges.' Jenny warned. She'd worked with Jack since Max had retired, but his reputation was well known. He didn't mince words or mess around. His pace and determination in investigating was respected by all.

'Her channel is called Cold Justice and she has a website too.'

'Williams.' Jenny started clicking keys and brought up the website and Youtube channel in two windows on her screen.

'She's worked on dozens of cases Boss. Her name online is Heather Jackson, not sure if it's her real name or not.'

'Get what you can and we'll pay her a visit. If she's holding back details on this case I want to know and she needs to give up her source or I'll charge her with obstruction.'

'Good luck with that.' Bridges mumbled and Jenny took a deep breath.

'You got something you want to share Bridges?'

'Sure. She's appeared before a magistrate four times and done time in support of her freedom to keep her sources secret.'

'Well number one, we don't live in the US and the right to keep a source from the police doesn't mean squat here, not if the judge deems it's in the public's best interest to know. And number two, if she's been to court and done time, she'll be on the records so finding her real name might have been hard for you Bridges, but I think we've got this.'

6

Jack opened the wrought-iron gate to a groan of protest from the sticky, rusted hinges. Following the red brick pavers to the concrete veranda, he reached a bright blue door that seemed overtly out of place against the bull-nosed roofline and heritage burgundy and green colour scene.

Jenny moved along as he knocked twice with enough force to wake the dead. 'Heather Jackson, Police! Open up!'

The sound of barking echoed down the hall but didn't draw any closer. Jack knocked harder, if that were possible. 'Jackson, we have a warrant to search the premises.'

Getting the warrant hadn't proved as difficult as Jack had anticipated. Judge Fellows had been more than accommodating once Jack outlined the circumstances to cease any and all evidence that might be pertinent to his investigation. It didn't hurt that he knew the Judge well through his father, but what really tipped the scales in his favour was the Judge's line on vigilante justice and rogue, inflammatory and misleading reporting by online bloggers. Not that Jack considered Jackson rogue, but working the way she did, she ran the risk of undermining police investigations.

The dog continued to yap, and Jack tried one last time to get Jackson to answer the door. The warrant didn't give them permission to enter without the reporter present. He looked at his watch, tapped his foot a moment, then moved down the veranda toward the front window.

Cupping his hand against the glass, he peered inside. Reaching for his gun, he moved back toward the door, Jenny instinctively became alert.

He indicated for her to draw her own weapon, which she did. He studied the door a moment before turning to her. 'Williams. Cover me.'

'That door looks pretty solid Boss,' she whispered, but stepped back a few paces and to the side.

He nodded. 'Wish Anderson was here with the super-fast pickpocket technique.' They'd both seen him unlock a door in a matter of seconds and Jack thought about getting him to share the skill next time they caught up.

Before barging his way in, Jack tried the door, which opened unhindered. He stood to the side and pushed it open a crack, to check if anyone was watching the door. With his heartbeat pounding in his ears, he waited. Nothing.

Pushing the door wide, he entered low and moved to the left through an archway, gun raised. 'Armed Police. Put your weapons down and hands up.' He sensed Williams move in behind him and caught sight of her in his peripheral vision as she moved to the right through another archway.

The hallway was eerie despite the now intense yapping sound coming from a closet in the hallway. Both detectives exchanged a glance. Jack pointed for Williams to go right, which led to a dining area, Jack continued to the left, into the formal lounge room.

'Clear.' He heard Williams call. Old heritage bungalows like this shared similar floorplans. Formal lounge off the hallway, dining through to the kitchen from the opposite side. The main hall led to all the bathrooms and bedrooms and ran down the centre of the home. In some cases. The kitchen opened back to the hallway.

'Clear,' he called, scanning the books strewn from the bookcase, the upturned coffee cup on the side table and the broken lamp on the floor as he re-entered the hallway and moved forward.

Williams joined him back in the hallway, having come out via the kitchen. She shook her head as they both moved down the wide walkway, the heritage fretwork arching over the transition hallway to back of the house.

Jack reached a bathroom on the left. The door was closed. The dog had stopped yapping and the silence grew uncomfortable. He reached up to the door handle and moved to open it, Williams covering him in case someone barged out past Jack.

The sound of a door slamming against the wall made them both jump back, but the door before them remained closed. It took a moment for them to realise where the sound had come from, by then the front door was slammed against the wall, the glass in the pane exploding with the force.

Jack turned and ran back to the front hall 'Stop! Police!' He didn't wait for Williams, she was either there or she wasn't. He'd worked with her long enough now to trust she'd back him up. Leaping from the veranda, without using the steps, Jack landed in a full run.

He stopped a moment, to see where their assailant had disappeared to, but the street was barren.

'Which way?' Williams drew up behind him.

'No idea. You go left, I'll go right.'

'Is that wise?'

'If they were armed, they would have shot at us already.' Williams nodded and did as she was told. Jack moved to the right, watching carefully as he passed a silver Mercedes, checking between it and the VW van pulled up behind. Three houses down he found a laneway, marked with bike lanes. There were two bright yellow bollards to prevent vehicle access.

Moving down the lane, he came to a park, full of play equipment and more bikeways going in various directions. He pulled out his mobile. 'Detective Cunningham. I need a Tracking

Dog Unit, 7 Parkway Drive Saint Peters.' He texted Williams to meet him back at the house, put his mobile back in his pocket before activating the safety on his weapon and returning it to his shoulder holster.

Williams was standing outside the rickety gate when he arrived back at the home of Heather Jackson.

'A Dog Unit is on the way, we need to clear the rest of the house.'

'The place has been ransacked.'

'I know. Let's hope whoever it was didn't find what they were looking for.' Jack reached the steps, pulled out a pair of gloves and put one on each hand. Williams did the same.

They ignored the rooms they'd already been through, but started at the now open closet in the hallway. Leaving the dog in the closet had seemed the best idea, but it had turned out to be a mistake. Their assailant had been hiding there, the dog barking until whoever had invaded the animal's home had suffocated it.

The terrier lay motionless, its dark brown eyes staring into space just inside the door of the closet. 'We'll get the K9 to start here.'

'What the hell!' Jack turned around to find a woman of medium height, with charcoal black hair, black eyeliner and glass black fingernails, standing defiantly with her hands on her hips in the hallway. Her expression showed no fear at the mess inside her home, but as her eyes dropped to the dead terrier, her expression became almost feral.

'I'm..'

'Declan. What happened to Declan?' She rushed forward, but Jack put his hand up to stop her. 'Who the hell are you?' Her voice had gone up an octave. 'What did you do to my dog!' She'd failed to fully take in the mess around her, her eyes focussed only on the animal inside the closet.

'Ms Jackson, I'm Detective Cunningham.' He reached for his badge. 'This is Detective Williams.' She looked at the badge closely, suspicion written all over her face.

'Okay. One question answered. Next!' She knelt near her dog, but Jenny had strategically placed herself between the dead animal and its owner.

'I'm sorry for your loss Ms Jackson, but you can't touch the dog...Declan right now.' Jack tried to be sympathetic. Animals had never been his thing, but he knew pet owners were often in as much shock over the death of an animal as of any human loved one.

'You've had a break in.' Jenny knelt next to the woman who had started to shake a little from the fleeing adrenalin.

'It's very fortunate you weren't home.' Jack added as he heard a siren in the distance. 'I have a Dog Unit on the way to see if we can find who did this. Whoever it was, they were still on the premises when we arrived.'

'What the...'

'We need to ask you some questions Ms Jackson, about the cold case you recently presented on Youtube.'

'You think this...' She wandered into the lounge-room, suddenly seeing the mess as she spoke, 'was because of the Marilyn De Beer case?'

'We'll explain our theories down at the station if that's alright with you?' Jack moved toward her.

'Am I under arrest?' Her posture became defensive.

'Absolutely not.' Jenny interrupted.

Jack knew he was being less sensitive than usual, but Marilyn's case had gotten to him way back when she first went missing. Now he *knew* he'd let her down, and maybe she'd been alive for a while before she was killed, he was beside himself with guilt.

'Look. We just need to process the scene. The station seems a good place for you to wait, but if you have somewhere else to stay, we can meet you at the station later, when you're ready to make a statement and answer some questions about the case you've been working on.'

Jenny was being far more diplomatic than Jack. He nodded for her to carry on, and moved away to assess the scene and meet the Dog Unit. The sirens outside had stopped, the whine of a dog and the firm voice of his handler, told him they were almost ready to get started.

He watched Detective Williams move outside with Ms Jackson as the German Shepherd reached the front step.

'Sergeant Stephens Sir, and this is Zac.' The German Shepherd pulled gently at his lead, waiting to begin the search. His intelligent eyes took in the scene as his tongued lolled from his mouth.

'In the closet, Sergeant. You'll find a deceased animal, likely suffocated by the assailant while he hid there.'

'That's fairly distressing Sir.'

'Will it interfere with the search, from the dog's perspective?'

'I don't think so Sir. Any idea which direction the assailant headed in?'

'I'm fairly certain they took off through the park about three doors down on the right, but let's see if Zac agrees.'

The handler nodded and moved toward the still open closet. The dog whined and showed mild distress a moment, but quickly focussed on the job set before him. Jack watched as the animal sniffed around in circles inside the closet, lifted its nose then moved out, down the hall to the front door and beyond.

He wasn't going to join the search. There were special police units to handle such things and it was likely they'd lose the trail as soon as the person got in a vehicle, but at least they'd know which street cameras to start running through to find a usable image.

He moved back out onto the veranda, re-joining his partner. 'You okay Jack?' They seldom used first names on the job, but they were friends outside the work environment, especially since Liz had roped them in on a number of her PI investigations. When Jenny used his first name, he knew she was genuinely concerned.

'I'm good Jenny. Let's focus on the investigation for now. Where's Jackson?'

'She's meeting us at the station after we've finished up here. She's provided an address where she'll be staying in case we need to speak with her before the interview and a phone number I can contact her on. She's been surprisingly cooperative, considering.'

'She wasn't exactly helping with her leak to the public.'

'I explained that to her Boss, but she said she thought the investigation had been shoved under a rock too long and that someone high up somewhere, was interfering with due process.'

'Well it isn't us.'

'She could just be a conspiracy nutter Boss, but I don't think so. She's broken some pretty hard-core cases in the past. I think we should treat her respectfully, and I think if we do, she'll reciprocate.'

'Let's hope so.'

7

Liz watched through the one-way glass, the view making her think of her interview with Bridges and the D.E.A. agent Moore when she was on the wrong side of the glass. The case had been a wakeup call in so many ways.

No more escort work for her, but also, no more casual liaisons with men who would just use her. Moore said he'd grown close to her, too close, but still, she felt like he'd used her to get the revenge he wanted for his wife and child's murder.

'Why did Jack want us here?' She watched the detective take a seat to the right of Ms Jackson. The desk wasn't a barrier, he was trying to keep her relaxed, but why the mirror, why the interrogation room?

'He wants us on this case with him Liz. It's going to be a tough ride for him.' Max looked at her and she spared him a quick glance, but her eyes quickly went back to the detective in front of her.

She'd been attracted to him the moment they'd met, and she thought he felt the same, but he'd never made a move to express his feelings. In fact, he'd turned down *any* hint of intimacy more than once and Liz wasn't exactly sure why.

Max had told her about this long-term relationship with Marilyn and how it had stopped Jack taking on any new serious relationships, but she was convinced it was *her* former career and the fact she was still the Madam of Adelaide's most successful escort agency that was holding him back. The problem was, she wasn't sure she could entirely quit the life, even for him and why should she have to?

'Ms Jackson. I'm not sure how you got wind of the details of this case, but I'm concerned you didn't come to us if you believe you have new evidence.'

'I've been looking into the disappearance of Marilyn De Beer for a number of years.'

Liz watched the young woman's body language. She was guarded, sitting back in her chair, her arms crossed over her chest. Her black nail polished fingers tapped an unheard rhythm on her elbow. Was she annoyed, or anxious? Liz couldn't be sure.

'Don't you usually only cover *unsolved* murders?' Liz could see Jack was struggling. His tone was calm, but she knew the detective well enough now to read his facial expression and he was stretched tighter than a bow string.

'I got a letter from a friend of hers, from South Africa who was worried Marilyn might have been murdered.'

'And you chose not to give that information to the police?'

'Forgive my bluntness detective, but weren't you Ms De Beer's boyfriend at the time of her disappearance?' Jack said nothing. Liz's stomach rolled. The same questions she'd had about Jack's closeness to the case were going to bite him in the butt now.

'You're hardly the right person to be investigating this case. Why are you allowed to follow up on your own girlfriend's murder? That's why I've not shared anything with the police.' Her tone was snarky, even a little immature.

'We don't know it was murder.' Jack almost whispered too quietly for them to hear.

'Sure you do. The pathologist and the anthropologist both agree she met with foul play.' Ms Jackson grinned at Jack's response, knowing she'd hit a nerve.

Liz sucked in a breath. The exact words the anthropologist used. 'How does she know that?' She looked to Max for an answer. He shrugged without taking his gaze from the interview room.

'I was given the option to lead this case *because* of my involvement Ms Jackson. I pursued this case right from the beginning. If I'd suspected for a second that Marilyn had been harmed, I would have never given up looking for her.'

'You would have had to be deaf and blind not to know she was in trouble.' Ms Jackson's tone was flat.

'Then I must have been both because I thought Marilyn was fine. Busy with her work, but fine.' Jack signed, sat back in his chair as his shoulders sagged.

'He's losing control of the interview. Where is Jenny?' Liz moved toward the door, but Max took her arm gently.

'Leave it to Jack. He's not stupid. Give him a second.' Max assured her but she didn't feel comfortable.

'If my chief thought I was involved, he would have pulled me from this case in a heartbeat. When Marilyn went missing I took a month of leave to try and find her. I've never taken leave Ms Jackson.'

The Youtube self-appointed reporter, commentator and investigator assessed Jack carefully. Liz watched her posture change, from squared off, away from Jack to shoulders facing him, arms unravelled from her chest and even adjusting her chair to face him.

She smiled to herself, 'She believes him.' Max grunted approval. Jack was deliberately trying to break down the barrier. The interview was in the interrogation room so Liz and Max could read Ms Jackson while Jack let her read him.

'I told you to give him a second. If she is going to open up about her source, the evidence she's found, she needs to be sure Jack wants justice as much as she does.'

'I read her website and watched her Youtube channel.' Liz watched the interview continue. 'Do you know why she does it?' Max shrugged as though he didn't really care. 'Her parents were killed when she was fifteen. Home invasion gone wrong they said, but she didn't believe it.'

'Let me guess. She solved the case.'

'No. But it started her on this path.'

'Tough nugget then.' Max didn't hide the admiration from his voice.

'I'd say so. I like her.'

'You would.' She smiled and returned her attention to the interview.

'Okay, let's say I believe you, that Marilyn was super good at hiding what she was up to. Why?'

'What do you mean?'

'Why didn't she tell her police boyfriend what she was investigating?'

'Marilyn was never one to share her concerns. Always kept her feelings bottled up. She was a hard woman to read.'

'Whoever broke into my place wouldn't have found anything.'

Jack's eyebrow rose. 'Why is that?'

'Because I don't keep anything at home, or on my laptop. I use an external server and they would need the log in details to access it.'

'How did you find out about Marilyn's cause of death?'

'It's not relevant. What is relevant is that her friend in South Africa said that just before her disappearance, she'd been investigating something to do with diamonds.'

'Diamonds?' Jack looked at the one-way glass and Jackson saw before he averted his eyes.

'Who's behind the glass? The other detective?' Her tone was calm but Liz could tell Jack was going to have to come clean or Ms Jackson wasn't going to continue cooperating.

'I have a consulting PI company helping me on this case. Just to ensure I'm above reproach and that my personal feelings don't cause any issues.' Jackson turned, her chair scraping the hard vinyl flooring as she peered through the glass.

'I'll introduce you, if you like?'

8

'You're an escort.' It wasn't a question and Liz tensed. 'That's awesome.' The tension eased. She grinned at the young woman. The dark hair, eyeliner and nails were not what made her remarkable to Liz. There was something in her eyes that reached out and grabbed a hold, before you could do anything to stop them.

'I'm retired.' Liz studied Jack's face as she spoke. 'I'm a full-time PI these days. This is my partner, Max Fitzpatrick.' Max shook the woman's hand and Liz watched her infectious smile, getting the impression she didn't let many people see it often.

Her short haircut was professional, trimmed back hard against the back of the neck much like Liza Minelli often wore. 'How did you become a PI?' The younger woman sat in a chair next to Liz to the right of Jack's desk in the main office. Jenny sat at her desk opposite Jack's, Max perched on the edge of Jack's desk.

'It's a long story.' And one Liz wasn't about to elaborate on just yet.

Liz saw Bridges watching their little meeting from across the room, the desk across from him still vacant. She wondered when the department would find a new detective to replace Rickard or Johnnie—another case she'd managed to get mixed up in that resulted in someone dying. She hoped there would be no new body count as they unravelled what happened to Marilyn De Beer.

'He looks lonely,' Liz spoke quietly into Jack's ear.

'He likes it that way.' Jack's breath made her skin tingle and her stomach roll as he whispered against her ear.

'So you work together on cases sometimes?'

'Strictly, that's not quite how it works. PI cases are often not criminal, but occasionally we end up on the same team.' Liz wanted to draw the focus away from her and Jack's working relationship because it was far from orthodox. 'Tell us how you got involved in this case Heather. You don't mind if I call you Heather?'

'As long as you don't mind if I call you Liz.' Those chocolate brown eyes were sharp and Liz nodded.

'I got that letter from a woman in Botswana.'

'Taiwo?' Liz looked at Max.

'Yes. You know her?' Heather looked surprised.

'We found old letters amongst Marilyn's personal possessions from Taiwo. They were nearly twenty years old. We hadn't had a chance to cross-reference email, phone or other information yet.'

'Carry on thanks Heather,' Jack encouraged. 'When was this first letter?'

'It was a few years ago. I contacted her by email to find out what she was concerned about. Then I did a little digging, hit a brick wall much like you most likely did and Taiwo stopped pushing me about the case. But then her bones came to light and I knew I needed to ramp it up.' Jack nodded, a sadness in his eyes made Liz reached for his hands, which were tightly clasped in his lap.

The gesture was quick, but he smiled and Heather's eyes said she was watching carefully.

'I pulled out my notes, went through them and started digging into the diamond stuff.'

'You said Taiwo mentioned diamonds.' Liz sat forward.

'Yes. She said Marilyn was asking about ethical diamond registration and audit procedures. Taiwo works for a diamond exporter. Of course, if you want to guarantee an ethical diamond, you need to get it from Canada or buy a lab grown one because the audit and documentation of ethical diamonds is a crock of shit.'

Max chuckled but Jack's brow furrowed. 'What do you mean?'

'Well, like any audit, you just have to tick boxes to say you've complied. There are pretty much no checks and balances in place to make sure each stage of the diamond production and exportation is really monitored.'

'Did Taiwo have any specifics on Marilyn's line of enquiry?' Liz watched Jack as he asked the question. She could see in his eyes that he felt responsible, like he should have known his girlfriend was running some sort of investigation.

'No. I'm guessing she didn't have enough evidence yet to bother you.' Heather offered him an out but he wasn't taking it.

'Still, why wouldn't she have cut me in on the investigation so I could be her back up?'

'Maybe she was only stabbing in the dark? What I want to know is what tipped her off? Why start the investigation?' Liz looked at the group for answers.

'You said you found diamond ring pics in her stuff?' Max suggested.

'Were you looking at getting engaged Jack?' Liz turned to him, trying to keep the question professional but somewhere deep inside, she knew she wanted to know just how serious their relationship had been.

'Not seriously. We were both in the midst of developing our careers. I'd just made detective and she was a few years from being able to practise accountancy in her own firm.'

'So she wouldn't have been looking at diamond rings for herself?' Liz pushed.

'I don't think so. Marilyn wasn't even big on jewellery. She'd grown up in South Africa. Her parents owned and ran an animal reserve for tourists. She liked the simple life, more a no shoes, farm kind of girl at heart. Other than a signet ring from her family and plain studs, she wore no jewellery.'

'So that leaves her work. Time to get a warrant and dig into all her past clients, accounts and work associates.' Max chimed in.

'We've been trying. *Guild and Glover* have been far from accommodating and I'm not sure we've got enough to get a judge to issue a warrant.'

'I might be able to help there.' Liz smiled and Jack frowned. 'I know a few people.'

'I bet you do.' Max teased, but Jack wasn't smiling.

9

Jack pulled the sheet from the murder board he'd covered while Heather was in the office. A picture of Marilyn was taped to the centre. To the right, he'd scribbled *Guild and Glover* earlier in the day. He now added the name *Gregory* with an arrow below the firm's name.

'What are you thinking?' Jenny stood back to watch her boss work.

'I'd like to know who leaked Marilyn's autopsy details to Heather, but I guess it doesn't really matter now.' He drew a line to the left of Marilyn's picture and wrote *ethical diamonds* next to it. 'What do you make of her now?'

He turned to Jenny, who took a deep breath before answering. 'I think she's genuine about solving crimes, not just making money from her Youtube channel and website.'

'Someone killed her dog and broke into her home. They think she knows something and it can't just be about Taiwo. Liz and Max were already on the friend's trail. What isn't she telling us?'

'Do you want me to organise surveillance?' Jenny pulled her mobile from her pocket.

'I'll get Max onto it.'

'Who's footing the bill for *Fox Investigations* on this one?'

'I am. I know I'll have to convince Liz to bill me, but I'll talk to her tonight about it. I want to go over Marilyn's things with her. I can't believe I missed the letters.'

'You were upset when she went missing. It's understandable.'

'Not really. I contacted her parents, left a message and asked them if they'd heard from her, but they never returned my calls.'

'And that didn't seem strange?'

'I got the impression Marilyn moving away was the ultimate betrayal because Marilyn never spoke to her family. Not even a phone call for special occasions.'

'But surely when she went missing they flew out to check on her?'

'You'd think so, but they didn't.' Jack opened his flip phone and dialled Max's number. There was no answer, so he texted a message with Heather's temporary address and a quick explanation. Putting the phone back in his pocket he sat down on the edge of the desk and stared at the white board, pinching his top lip between thumb and forefinger reflexively.

They didn't have much. He moved forward and ran his hand over the photo of Marilyn's skull fracture. His hand drifted to the head shot photo. Marilyn had been beautiful, with full lips, blonde hair and bronze legs that went on forever, but she'd always been a closed book to him.

He'd liked it that way. Too much emotion was just distracting from his career. The sex was good, the company was fun but now as he considered their relationship he realised he'd never really loved Marilyn. Love was about messy emotions. Love meant you were worried about someone, excited to see them, focussed on their happiness and connected to them in a way that you couldn't explain.

A petite, feisty brunette came to mind and Jack's stomach lurched. Liz was going to infiltrate *Guild and Glover* using her past connections and the idea brought back memories of their first case together when Liz's best friend and fellow escort had been found murdered.

Liz had moved heaven and earth to reveal Becca's killer, including seducing Malcolm Light to uncover a connection between the Adelaide socialite and his own corrupt father, Judge Cunningham. The fact his dad turned out dirty was a shock, but what had really disturbed him and still did, was Liz's willingness to use her sex-appeal to get what she wanted.

It wasn't his place to challenge her choices, but every time she succumbed to the temptation, he had to distance himself emotionally. He wasn't sure how much longer he could do it, or if he ultimately should.

****

Liz put her bag on the counter. She was glad Jack had called her in to watch the interview with Heather. The girl was a firecracker and Liz considered bringing her on as an investigator, depending on how this case panned out.

She walked around the counter to her wine fridge and pulled out a fresh bottle of Pinot Grigio. Placing the glass on the counter, she noticed the photos of Marilyn still sprawled out. Ignoring them, she considered how she was going to catch up with Richard Glover.

He was an old client whom she'd stopped seeing some time ago. Striking up a relationship with him wasn't impossible and could be very lucrative for their investigation, but something was niggling in the back of her mind.

Her eyes fell on a photo of Jack with Marilyn and Liz knew what the irritation was. Jack was a monogamous type of guy and deep down she craved the kind of intimacy that came from a long-term relationship, but the temptation to use her connections was addictive—like kicking a drug she knew was bad for her, but she just couldn't shake the hold.

Ted's face popped into her head. She smiled as she thought about their last night together. Her high-heels, the lustful looks she'd felt at her back from the men in the bar as she walked towards Ted, who stood to greet her. It was empowering to know she wielded that sort of control over men. Then Ted's face was replaced by his crime scene photo—a bullet hole in his forehead, his naked body limp and grey.

Her phone pinged with a text. *I'll come by tonight and go over Marilyn's effects if you don't mind.*

She looked at Jack's message and wondered over how she felt about reliving his past relationship, but typed the reply she knew he needed.

Seven is good.

Done. See you then.

Still tossing up exactly how she was going to handle Richard Glover, she opened her laptop and began typing an email. The meeting could go two ways, and Liz hoped Richard didn't choose the wrong way.

10

Liz sipped her wine as she stirred the chicken curry. Her mind was running around in circles over Richard Glover's email response. He sounded horny, even via email and that concerned her.

The door buzzer made her jump, her wine sloshed over the side of the glass in response. She placed it on the counter and grabbed a tea-towel, moving to the door, then stopped, returned to her security camera footage and double-checked it was Jack. Her years on the street had made her tough, but wise and a woman alone could never be too complacent.

A few seconds passed as she viewed the screen, ensuring it was Jack arriving at seven as agreed. She was still wiping the wine from her hand when she opened the door.

'Good evening.' Jack handed her a bottle of wine, a shy smile curled his lip.

'You didn't have to.' She took it and moved aside, waving for him to enter. He'd never brought her wine before and the simple act seemed to change the mood in the room.

'I'm always drinking yours. It seemed polite.' He shrugged, an air of nervousness in the gesture.

'You want a glass? You're staying for dinner, right?' The air felt like it had been sucked out of the room and Liz puzzled over it. They'd work together for months, why was dinner and wine so awkward suddenly?

'I see you've been going through the photos.' Her question was answered. Jack's personal life was all over her living room and she still wasn't exactly sure why he'd asked for her help on this case.

'Dinner. Are you staying?' He seemed distracted.

'Oh, sorry, if that's okay?'

'Of course. Did you want to help yourself to a wine? I'm just finishing up here.' Liz opened a drawer and took out two large white plates ready to dish up.

'Thanks.' Jack moved into the kitchen, reaching over Liz to the cupboard where her wine glasses lived. She ducked out of his way, her hair brushing against his five o'clock shadow and catching like Velcro.

He stopped reaching, looked down at her as she moved to look up at him, their faces only inches apart. 'Sorry. I'm straight from work.' His words were almost a whisper.

'All good. Nothing like a little Clooney or George Michael bristle to make the ladies swoon.' She quickly looked back at the frying pan on the stove top, wondering why on earth she'd said such a stupid thing.

'Do you need a refill?'

'Yes.' Too quickly. 'Thanks.' Jack moved away and Liz felt like she could finally breathe again. Reaching out for the cooked rice, she began serving up dinner as Jack put the wine away and took her glass to the kitchen counter.

'Heather is an interesting one.' He fidgeted with his wine glass.

'She is. Running an investigation into unsolved murders or missing persons is a unique role for such a young woman.'

'Max said you knew her parents died.'

'I do my homework Detective.' She smiled seductively and quickly focussed back on serving the food.

'We back to detective again.'

'Only when you challenge my PI skills.' It was his turn to smile.

'Wouldn't dream of it. You've proven yourself.'

'Is that why you wanted me helping with Marilyn's case?' Liz pushed Jack's plate across the counter to where he'd taken a seat. She collected cutlery and joined him. He'd remained silent, turning his wine glass around in a slow circle.

'I asked you to help with Marilyn's case for two reasons. One, I think you can help, you have a nose for solving the seemingly unsolvable.' He took a sip of his wine, placed the glass down and busied himself with moving his plate and picking up his fork.

'And number two?' she coaxed.

'Number two I've not entirely worked out myself yet.'

'But you know there is another reason.' Liz wanted to reach out and stroke his rough jawline.

'You shared your past with me. It was only polite to return the favour.' It wasn't the answer she'd been hoping for and something in his crystal blue eyes told her it wasn't the reason he had in mind either, but he wasn't ready to share.

He put a forkful of curry into his mouth and moaned. Liz couldn't help wondering what it would be like to make him moan for a totally different reason than her food. A grin slipped across her face, one that made Jack's eyebrows rise, but he looked away.

They ate in silence for a few minutes. The occasional sideways glance from Jack made it obvious he was feeling the strange vibe as much as she. He finally lifted his wine, took a sip and broke the silence.

'How's Jackie doing now she's finished her bar exams?

'Good. She's working full-time at her dad's firm now but she really wants to break out on her own sometime, just not sure what and when.'

'It was nice to finally meet her, but your kidnapping crime scene wasn't really the best place to be introduced for the first time.'

Liz chuckled. 'I don't know, you made a good impression.'

'I did?' Jack rose to pack his plate away in the dishwasher. Liz knew him well enough to know he didn't like things left untidy or unfinished.

'Leave it. I'll clean up.' Liz placed her hand on his arm to encourage him to return to his seat. 'We have Marilyn's things to go over. I went through them, but if you think I might have missed something, we can go over them together.'

He looked at her hand, then a pile of photos on the end of the counter caught his eye. He reached out and pulled them closer. 'I forgot about these. When I couldn't find her, I didn't want to see them again so I just packed them away and tried to forget.'

'You loved her a lot?' Liz wasn't sure if it was a question or a statement but the look in Jack's eyes shared his pain.

'I don't know if I loved her, really. I've been thinking about it a lot since I got the case report.' He flicked through the photos one by one. Liz got up to move the dishes, leaving him to his memories a moment.

'Liz, I wanted you on this case with me because I need you. I wasn't going to say anything.' He fell silent, his eyes still on the stack of photos in front of him. Liz left the dishes, returning to the seat next to him.

She wanted to reach out and kiss him, to tell him she needed him too, but words just wouldn't leave her lips. She thought of Ted, of Richard and his horny email and something told her Jack was still never going to understand.

'Jenny told me you've stopped working.' They both knew which work he was referring to. 'I...'

'What Jack?' She needed him to say it. She couldn't explain why but in every client relationship, she was the Madam, the Boss. She just couldn't be that person in this relationship. This had to be led by Jack.

'We better go over this case, make sure we've covered everything in Marilyn's personal effects.' Liz sighed. Hot tears burnt the back of her eyes, but she did what she'd learnt to do as a kid—when Les had snuck into her room while her mum slept. She swallowed her emotions deep down, the physical pain almost making her want to throw up her entire meal.

'Okay, let's start with the letters from Taiwo. I've traced the delivery address.' She picked up a letter and handed it to Jack. 'It's not yours, so the letters were exchanged before Marilyn moved in with you, but we guessed that from the post mark dates.'

'We only moved in together when Marilyn finished university and started working for *Guild and Glover*.'

'And that was?' Liz moved to the dining table, collected her laptop which usually lived on her counter, but she'd moved it for dinner. Opening her dot point list, she added next to Marilyn's earlier address a dash and waited for the reply.

'Just before Christmas two-thousand and eight. She lived in Semaphore before that.' He waved the envelope in the air. 'Not this address. I'll get Jenny to run a check and see if it's relevant.'

'The letters are nearly twenty years old. Was Marilyn here in her twenties?'

'I don't know? We never spoke much about our past. She knew I didn't want much to do with my dad and I knew she didn't speak to her family. The past wasn't a big discussion point for us.'

Liz decided to let the subject drop for now. Where Marilyn lived when she was in her twenties was unlikely to bear any relevance to her death anyway, but Jack would run the address and see if anything important came up.

'Did Marilyn help you redecorate?' She smiled at his surprised expression.

'How did you know?'

'I wondered if a woman's hand was involved the very first time I saw inside your apartment.'

'She had a flare for it. I often wondered why she'd chosen accountancy over interior design.'

'Probably the money I'd say.' Liz typed the date into the computer and waited for Jack to open the first box.

'You said she had photos of diamond rings?'

'Magazine articles, yes, in the other box.' She pointed to the second clear plastic box. 'You packed the boxes up, you didn't notice?'

'I wasn't paying that much attention to be honest. I packed them up after the month I'd taken leave to try and find her.'

'Max told me you asked him to stake out where Heather is staying.'

'Sorry, should I have checked in with you first?' Jack's tone said he didn't think it was necessary and Liz told herself it didn't matter, but she didn't answer him. 'She's up to something.'

'I like her.'

'She's still hiding something. Her place was trashed. What she told us was all over mail, or email discussions but the drawers were pulled out. The dog killed to keep it quiet. The cushions cut open, the cupboards emptied. Whoever they were, they were looking for something and it wasn't an email chain.'

'You think she's in danger?' Jack didn't say anything but his expression spoke volumes. 'Good thing Max is keeping an eye on her then.'

'Speaking of danger. Are you seeing someone close to *Guild and Glover*?'

'I'm seeing Richard Glover tomorrow night.'

'At night, does it have to be at night?'

'Why?' Liz watched Jack carefully, his posture had changed, his face almost a grimace.

'Nothing.'

'What?'

'Nothing, really, I should go. I think I've checked everything I need to.'

'You haven't gone through all the boxes.'

'I trust you.'

'Are you sure?' Liz had a pretty good idea what had changed Jack's focus on Marilyn's personal belongings and it had nothing to do with how thoroughly she'd gone over them.

'It's late. I've got an early start.' Jack moved toward the door.

'I give up Jack. You know I'm not taking new clients and you know I've let all my clients go too.' Liz felt like throwing something.

'You didn't have to do that.' He spoke quietly.

'Of course I fucking did and still you look at me like a whore.'

'Liz I don't think of you like that at all.'

'Just go Jack.' Liz couldn't hold the tears any longer. She wasn't sure if it was the wine, or the fact Jack said he'd never loved Marilyn or was it that she couldn't decide if sleeping with Richard Glover was going to give her what she wanted or not.

'I'm not going anywhere.' He moved toward her.

'Leave me alone.' She turned and moved toward her bedroom, the tears were rolling down her cheeks now and she didn't want him to see her cry. To see her weak.

'Liz.' He followed her. 'I'm sorry. I'm a wanker.' He reached out and grabbed her wrist, but she wrenched her arm free and kept walking.

'I have no right to ask you to give up your work.' Liz stopped, her arm resting on the entrance way to the hall leading to her bedroom, her sanctuary. 'Or to dictate who you see.'

She turned. 'Or who I have sex with?' She watched him cringe, but she needed him to understand that she couldn't give up her life without knowing where they stood. 'If you want me all to yourself Detective, you have to tell me you want me. Do you understand!'

Jack opened his mouth, closed it, opened it again but nothing came out. Liz turned and took another step toward her room. He was behind her, his arm wrapped around her waist, his chest firm against her before she could take another breath.

'I want you Liz Jeffreys.' His words were hot in her ear, the rough whiskers of his chin bristly against her cheek. Liz turned slowly, Jack moved her against the wall, his hand slowly caressed her lower back.

She touched her finger to his jawline, tracing it slowly to his lower lip which was so close to hers that she could feel each breath on her skin. 'I like the sound of that.'

'I want you so much that it makes me do stupid things, say stupid things.'

'Stop talking.' She brushed her lips against his.

'This is going to get complicated.' His lips touched hers, softly, gently.

'You have no idea.' Jack's hand moved down her back, over her backside and pulled her body in close.

11

Jenny clicked keys on her computer as Jack updated details on the whiteboard. 'Did you find a connection between Marilyn, her work and the dump site?'

'Nothing yet. You were in early this morning.' Jenny looked up, lifted her cup of coffee and saluted. 'Thanks for the coffee.'

'You're welcome.' Jenny's eyes questioned the lack of explanation to his early start. Jack turned back to the whiteboard, saying nothing. Liz and he had agreed to keep their personal life just that, between the two of them, for now at least.

'I've been researching ethical diamonds though. Apparently all diamonds from South Africa were technically conflict diamonds up until the year two-thousand when the Kimberley Process was developed and instigated.'

Jack returned his attention to Jenny as she scanned her computer screen for information. 'Since then, ethically sourced diamonds have undergone a custody protocol to ensure no proceeds go to finance civil war or warlords in Botswana.'

'So Marilyn's friend Taiwo—who we assume is a long standing friend judging by the letters that pre-date our relationship—works for one of these companies that tracks the custody of the diamonds.'

'Yep.'

'And Marilyn contacted her for information.' Jack rubbed his chin and moved back to the murder board, adding Taiwo's name with an arrow down from the words *Ethical Diamonds*. 'Do we know what company she works for?'

'No, but I'll do a search and see what I can find. Maybe we need to make a call to South Africa?'

'We can try, but she might not take our call. We also don't want to tip anyone off, she or her work might be involved. Do we know anyone who can help? Maybe put a tail on Taiwo?'

'I don't know. Would Marilyn's parents be able to talk with Taiwo?'

'I don't think that's a good idea. They cut off all contact with Marilyn when she moved to Australia and when she went missing, they didn't exactly jump on the next plane.'

Jenny frowned. 'Should we be looking at them as suspects?'

Jack thought about it a moment, the felt tip marker pen still hovering over the whiteboard. 'Let's check with immigration and see if they came into Australia in the past eleven years.'

'I'll ask Anderson. He can probably get that sort of info a lot faster than me.'

'Good idea. If this goes international, we'll need his help. He might be able to put us in contact with someone to watch Taiwo.'

'I'll call now.' Jenny pulled out her mobile and tapped the screen to show her recent calls. Since she'd moved into her unit overlooking Hindmarsh Square, she'd seen a lot more of the federal police officer than before. He lived with his mum—her dementia requiring his attention, but when he could get a night away, he spent it with her.

'That's a caller ID I can't ignore.' Hemi's voice was deep and the tone laced with enough sex appeal to curl her toes.

'Sorry but this is a business call.' She tried to keep her voice even, but she knew Hemi could hear the quaver.

'Tonight okay with you?'

'Yes.' Jenny looked up self-consciously, only to find Jack busy back with the murder board, adding Heather's name next to Taiwo's with an arrow back to Marilyn's photo in the middle of the board.

'Good. What's up?'

'I need to run a few names through immigration records and it's a bit time sensitive. Do you know anyone who can speed up the process?'

'For you babe, of course. Shoot me an email and I'll get it fast tracked.' There was a short silence. 'Six okay with you?'

His Kiwi accent on the word six made her take a moment to reply. 'Your accent threw me a second.' He laughed. *Sex okay with you* was a pretty loaded question.

'I'll take a yes on either option.' She blushed, hoping Jack's eyes were still on the whiteboard.

'I'll see you then, and I'll send the details through now. Thanks.'

'Always a pleasure.' He hung up and Jenny stared at the phone a moment before putting it on the desk.

12

Max found stakeouts the worst for his dying smoking habit. He'd managed nearly five months without a smoke, but sitting in a car, snapping photos was tedious work and it was when he used to smoke the most. He'd managed without nicotine gum since Liz's kidnapping, but today was making him restless.

He reached inside his glove compartment, searching for some gum. An empty bright pink paper bag, the cinnamon and sugar from long gone donuts spilled to the passenger's side floor.

'Damn.' His new car had lost the new car smell months ago, but Liz would wring his neck if he let it turn into the hovel that was his home. He was saving for new digs. Liz paid well, but still, his background had been less than clean and he'd had a few unpaid debts to sort out before he could rent a new apartment.

The goth chick was growing on him, but Jack still didn't trust her and his instincts were solid in Max's book, so he was taking the surveillance seriously. He looked at his watch and ignored his grumbling stomach. Lunch was going to have to wait today.

The front door of the warehouse apartment opened and his target pulled the door closed, a black backpack on her back, her Doc Martin boot laces hanging free. She moved down the road and Max sighed as it became obvious she wasn't getting in a car.

Shrugging off his bad mood, he consoled himself with the fact he needed the exercise anyway. Heather moved around the corner and Max jumped out, pressed the lock button on his keys and shoved them into the pocket of his faded blue jeans. He was still getting used to wearing casual clothing instead of a full suit and as summer was just around the corner, he was considering shorts, something he'd never been able to wear as a detective.

He jogged up to the corner and peered around to see Heather posting something in a red mailbox on the footpath. She pulled out her phone before carrying on down the street. The black van came from a side street. Max's skin crawled the moment he spotted it.

Pushing his walk to a full run, he watched in horror as the side door opened and an assailant with broad shoulders and a balaclava leant out to reach for Heather.

'Get down.' He screamed as he drew his weapon. Heather turned, too late. The hooded figure grabbed her around the waist, lifting her feet from the roadside. Max shot at the door, not wanting to risk hitting Heather. A second shot rang out a moment later, smashing the glass window on the sliding door.

Heather thrashed and screamed as her legs left the pavement. Max closed the distance as the van slowed to allow the occupants a chance to wrangle their prey into the vehicle. He stopped, planted his feet firmly and took one last shot as a second figure tried to pull the door closed with Heather's legs still hanging half out, her feet dragging along the road, the soles of her Docs leaving a black trail on the bitumen.

The shot hit the first figure in the top of his shoulder, blood sprayed and Heather fell to the roadside, rolling once as Max took a moment to read the registration number before putting his legs into top gear to reach Heather.

His phone was in one hand, his gun in the other as he called for paramedics. He reached Heather moments later, placed his phone on speaker and laid it on the ground next to her head. Lifting her head gently, he inspected her for injuries and waited for the operator to answer.

Max struggled for breath, his heart racing, the sound drumming in his ears. 'You're gonna be okay.' Heather's eyes rolled back as she slipped from consciousness and the operator finally picked up.

13

Max saw Jack out the corner of his eye before his former partner entered the room. His body language spoke volumes, but even Max was surprised by the level of frustration in his words.

'What the fuck were you thinking!'

'Easy Jack.' Max soothed.

'I'm an investigative journalist, it's what I do.' Heather was no pushover and now that the shock of her attack had worn off, along with the pain medication, she was angry and frustrated.

'No, you're just a kid snooping into crimes that you don't know anything about!'

'I'm twenty-one.'

'You're a twenty-one-year-old with a chip on your shoulder is what you are.' Jack's voice was loud enough to bring a nurse running.

'Detective. I must…' Jack put his hand up to stop her talking before storming out of the room.

The nurse surveyed the temperature in the room, nodded and returned to her station.

'He's a wanker.'

'At times, but he's a good cop and do you know why?' Max stood at the foot of Heather's bed, the curtains were open and light streamed in through the window of her private room.

'I don't care.'

'Yes, you do.'

'Why then?' Her tone was petulant and Max grinned at the irony of Jack's statement. She was just a kid, who'd lost her parents at fifteen and wanted answers to all the world's problems.

'Because he cares, just like you do, about all the cases he works on. You have more in common than you realise.'

Heather huffed and looked out the window. Max could see her mind was elsewhere. On the case, on her parent's death, on her near-miss maybe.

'He's going to want to know what you have on this case that's so important someone would try to grab you like that.' Silence. 'You scared the shit out of me you know.'

Her eyes met his. 'I spoke with Taiwo a few weeks ago.'

Max sat back on the chair by her bedside. 'I think you should tell Jack.'

'Tell me what?' Jack moved back into the room, Heather gave him the stare of death. 'Look, I'm sorry. I over-reacted.'

'You think.' Max gave her a half-hearted warning with his eyes, she shrugged it off. 'Alright, maybe I should have told you before.'

'You think.' Jack smiled to soften the blow. 'I want to solve this case. I know you do too. We need to know everything you know Heather.'

Her dark eyes studied Jack, then flicked to Max as she took a deep breath and composed herself. Max wondered if the breath was just part of her trying to give herself time to come up with another half-truth or not. There was something in her eyes that told him she wasn't exactly accustomed to team work.

'Taiwo hadn't taken my calls or replied to my emails in ages. It was like she had decided to give up on the case and I had to admit, I'd put it on the back burner myself. But I sent her a message to say Marilyn's body had been recovered and she freaked. I think maybe she thought Marilyn had just skipped out to be safe from whatever she had uncovered, but knowing she was dead made it all too real.'

'What did she tell you?' Jack moved to the end of the bed and sat down on the crisp white sheets next to Heather's leg.

'She told me that Marilyn had been asking questions before she went missing. Questions about her parents' resort and why one of her clients might be paying them money.'

'Which client?'

'She didn't tell Taiwo, or maybe Taiwo isn't talking but Marilyn's parents owning a resort in Botswana. Why would one of Marilyn's clients be paying them money?'

'That's a good question. It could be just as simple as a holiday, but then why would it have sparked her interest? I think it's time to push for that warrant with *Guild and Glover* even if they don't like it.' Jack stood up from the bed, his phone in his hand as he headed out of the room.

Max looked back at Heather a moment before following Jack out. 'Isn't Liz organising to meet someone from *Guild and Glover* already? They will just lawyer up and organise an injunction on the grounds of client confidentiality if we push them.'

'Maybe Liz won't have to. We need to get a hold of Taiwo and get a statement. All we have is hearsay right now.'

'I got a rego number on the vehicle, probably stolen plates, but worth checking.'

'I better get an official statement from both of you.'

'What are we going to do with her when the hospital discharges her?'

'You two seem to have hit it off. Why not take her to your place?'

'I have a one bedroom apartment, you've got three. Why not your place?'

'Because I'm still a cop and I can't take a witness to a crime I'm investigating, home with me.'

'Maybe Liz will take her.'

'Unlikely. She likes her privacy.'

'Damn.'

'You know she's holding something back right.' Jack pulled a pad and pen out of his pocket ready to return to the room and take Heather's statement.

'She's guarded, but I'm not sure it's because she's keeping anything from us.'

'Do you really think someone would try to snatch her from the street for that little tidbit of information she told us? And you didn't see her home Max. They left no stone unturned mate. It was trashed—torn cushions, toppled bookcases. She's got something else they want.'

'My place it is then.'

'Jack.' Jenny moved toward them in the corridor.

'What you got Williams?' Jack put his pen and paper away in his jacket pocket as the junior detective drew closer.

'Anderson traced the De Beers. It seems they've been to Australia sixteen times in the past eleven years.'

'That doesn't make any sense. They never once visited Marilyn, or tried to contact me about her disappearance.'

'Top of the suspect list then?'

'I'm not sure, but definitely worth contacting. We'll try phoning them. Any luck finding someone in South Africa to interview Taiwo, discretely?'

'Not yet. Anderson is calling in a few favours.'

'Okay, great. I need to take Heather's statement. Can you take Max's?'

'Sure.'

Jack moved back into Heather's room, his pen and pad back out ready. She looked vulnerable sitting up in bed, her black eyeliner smudged, a broken black fingernail on her right index finger and a bruise forming on her left cheek.

'You ready to make a statement?'

'If I have to.' The body language was defiant but the voice lacked conviction.

'You probably should tell your friend, the one who owns the warehouse, that you were traced back to their address.'

'Shit!' She reached for her phone.

'Is your friend at work?'

'He works from home.'

'Handy.' Jack watched Heather bite her fingernail as she waited for her friend to answer. 'Do you need me to send a uniformed officer around?'

'No.' Too quick.

'What's up Heather?'

'Nothing.' Still too quick. 'Jeremy is a little eccentric, that's all.'

'Really? Does he know anything about your investigation? Could he be in danger?'

'Pick up.' She spoke to the unanswered phone at her ear. Hanging up, she tapped out a text message. Jack couldn't see what was written, and Heather's fingers moved too fast for him to track the key movement.

'Look Heather. I like you, I want to believe you, but so far you've been less than fully cooperative.'

'Not now.'

'Heather!' Jack slapped his pad down on the hospital table that sat over her bed. She jumped, her eyes boring into his as she sent her text and waited for a reply.

'What.' Her voice was ominously quiet.

'I understand you want to see this investigation through. I'm sure Liz will be willing to let you join her team while they work, but your house has been ransacked. Every cushion, cupboard and drawer ripped open. Now someone has tried to kidnap you. I've been willing to wait on you to trust me, but if you have another person involved and they are in danger…'

'Jeremy helps me out with computer stuff.'

'Like Microsoft Word or something less mainstream.' She rolled her eyes.

'What do you think?'

'I think you need to stop with the games.'

Heather looked at the unanswered screen of her phone and took a long slow, shuddering breath. She was just about to say something when the phone pinged. Jack swore under his breath as Heather frantically typed out a reply.

'I can get a warrant for that phone you know.'

'Good luck with that.' She put it behind her pillow and crossed her arms.

'If your friend ends up harmed, I'm charging you.' She scowled. 'Now... statement.'

****

'Get a uniform car over to the warehouse. Run an address check and find out who lives there. All Heather said was Jeremy someone.'

'What's up?' Jenny pulled her phone out and dialled.

'Whoever she was staying with is doing something to help her with her investigation. Either this one, or another one and she isn't sharing but she was worried about them until they replied to a text.'

'Got it.' She held up her finger as someone answered the phone.

'You done with your statement Max?'

'Yep, gave Williams the rego number so she can try and trace the van. Do you want me to head over to the warehouse and check on her friend?'

'No, we'll get a uniform unit on it for now.' He turned to Williams. 'Just get him to answer the door so we can tick it off the list, but I want to know who he is.' She nodded as she spoke into her phone.

'Probably a boyfriend.'

'I don't think so.'

'How'd you go with Liz last night?' Max joined Jack as they both made their way out of the hospital.

'What do you mean?' Jack looked at Max, trying to see what he was getting at, but there was nothing accusatory about his ex-partner's expression. He let out a breath.

'What did you think I meant?' Max rubbed his chin, a sly grin spreading across his face. 'Oh!'

'Oh! What?'

'Secret's safe with me mate.' Max tapped his nose. 'Nudge, nudge, wink, wink. I got your back.'

'Oh shut up. Are you taking Miss Congeniality home to your place then?' He needed to change the subject.

'Sure. When the doc releases her. You got any dates yet on the concrete that covered Marilyn up?

'Yeah, Williams confirmed the concrete was laid a week after Marilyn disappeared. Whoever took her, killed her within that week.'

'You gotten more from forensics yet?'

'No, still waiting on soil, bug and other reports, but at least we have a clear timeline for her death now.'

'Anything the forensic team think might pan out.' Max knew the drill and Jack held out the same hope himself, but the team hadn't been hopeful.

'At this stage, I'm not expecting much. This is going to have to come down to getting a warrant for Marilyn's files from *Guild and Glover* and without a statement from Taiwo or some other sort of proof Marilyn found something in her work files that got her killed, we aren't likely to get one.'

'Liz will get that sorted.'

Jack tried not to think about it. He'd deliberately not discussed Glover with Liz. He'd finally taken the first step, even if he had almost botched it. When he'd seen her tears, he'd finally understood what everyone had been trying to tell him. Still, where it went from here was in her hands.

14

Liz touched up her lipstick, placing it back in her purse as the taxi rolled over the Torrens River bridge on King William Road. The Cathedral sat majestically, overlooking the lush parklands and Liz considered her dress choice for the meeting.

Wearing a silk shirt, fitted skirt and tailored jacket, she felt like she'd strategically set the tone. Changing the meeting to daytime, in his office, should help keep everything professional, and not in the escort sense. Now she only hoped Robert understood.

The taxi pulled up outside the North Adelaide office and Liz paid the driver, offering him a tip. He smiled broadly as Liz hopped out and took in the smoked glass fronted building. She thought her tastes leaned to the opulent, until she entered the foyer.

She approached the receptionist, who took in her attire from top to toe. 'May I help you?' The well-used smile and tone of a practised secretary made Liz chuckle inside, thankful she'd never had to work behind a desk.

'Liz Jeffreys to see Robert Glover, he's expecting me.' She'd advised Robert of her real name, not that her long standing former client didn't know, but Liz had been careful once again to create a clear boundary between her former profession and her new PI work.

'Certainly Ms Jeffreys, can I offer you a drink? Coffee, tea, sparkling water perhaps?'

'Water would be lovely, thank you.'

'Perfect, I'll show you through to the meeting room. Just follow me.' The receptionist stood up, her full height towering over Liz's five foot-four. The woman's six-inch stilettos served to elongate the line of her legs as her mid-thigh, pleated skirt flounced with every step.

Liz wondered if the woman might be interested in a career change. Just because she was out of the game herself, didn't mean there wasn't always room for new escorts at *Foxy* and this girl had the look.

'Thank you.' Liz took a seat at the small round glass table, with a cast stainless steel pedestal leg. The water appeared seconds later, as the receptionist smiled that fake smile Liz knew only too well.

'Mr Glover will be with you shortly, he's just finishing up with an online meeting that has run overtime.'

'All good.' The receptionist turned to leave. 'Actually, just on the off chance you're looking for a deviation from your usual work.' The woman's eyes opened wider in curiosity as Liz handed her a card. 'I know a few people who'd pay very handsomely for the company of a lady such as yourself. Please don't be offended if this isn't up your alley, but I just thought you might like to know you have options.'

The woman took the card, studying it a moment. Her expression went from shock, to an embarrassed grin and Liz had a good feeling she'd be getting a call.

'No pressure, just consider it. My website is on the card, take a look and see if this is your kind of career move or not. It isn't for everyone.'

'Thanks. I will have a look.' The receptionist had a spring in her step as she flounced a little more energetically out of the meeting.

Liz studied the décor, resisting the urge to check the emails on her phone. The palm in the corner was real. A wall of windows overlooked the parklands through tinted glass and Liz could see paddle boats on the river cruising past on the sunny spring day.

The chrome legged chair was comfortable, with soft leather, high back and sprung base. *Guild and Glover* were doing a roaring trade it seemed and must have garnished some high-end clients to sustain the rent of the building alone.

'Lillian.' Robert Glover entered, looking not a day older than the last time Liz had seem him.

'Liz.' She corrected him. 'Thanks for seeing me Robert.'

'Oh, sorry.' He looked over his shoulder conspiratorially and grinned. 'Old habits die hard.'

'It's fine. I'm still getting used to it myself.' She kissed his cheek in European style, once on each side not really touching lips to skin, just puckering and making a kissing kind of sound.

'Your email was very mysterious. What's this all about?' Liz had considered exactly how she was going to make this work for her. It was only a matter of time before everyone who ever knew Lillian became acutely aware of why she'd cancelled her client list and what career had triggered her retirement.

'Well you know I've retired, but you likely don't know why.' Robert took a seat as Liz smoothed her skirt and crossed her legs, taking a sip of her water before continuing. 'My best friend and fellow colleague was killed earlier in the year and I was heavily involved in the case to find the killer.'

'I'm so sorry. I didn't know.' Robert leant forward, touched Liz's hand, patting it in sympathy.

'We found her killer.'

'We?' Robert's eyebrows rose as high as the pitch of his voice.

'Yes. I worked with the Major Crimes detectives... long story but one of them is an old friend.' She opted for leaving her former marriage to Max out of the discussion. It was far too complicated to try and explain to everyone she met.

'That's convenient.' Robert leant back now, his legs crossed, fingers working up and down to make a church steeple.

'Yes, very. In the end, we solved Becca's murder and I kind of got a taste for working with the police.' She didn't mention exactly how that taste had led to her sleeping with one of the detectives. The previous night flooded her mind with images of Jack's rippling abs as she held his hips tightly between her legs, his hands cupping her breasts. For the first time in a long time she thought she might have blushed because Robert stopped to study her, his expression perplexed.

'Anyway, one thing has led to another and my old friend handed his detective badge in for a PI badge and he now leads investigations for my PI firm, *Fox Investigations*.' She handed him a card.

'Escort to PI. That's one hell of a leap.' He studied the card as he spoke, the crease between his eyebrows growing deeper by the second. 'So what has this to do with me, or *Guild and Glover*?'

'Look, I know a couple of detectives visited Tuesday, requesting some records and they hit a brick wall.' Richard crossed his arms over his chest. Liz read the sign. 'I have a deal sweetener.' A grin crossed his face and she knew where his mind was going. 'Not necessarily the type you're thinking but maybe just as attractive.'

'Go on.' He leant forward, his arms on the glass table now.

'I'll bring all my accountancy to your firm, at the right price of course. That's my *Foxy Escort Agencies,* my philanthropic trusts and my new PI agency, if you'll do me one favour.'

'Ask and I'll see if it's within my scope to comply.' Non-comital, he sounded like a lawyer, not an accountant.

'A little over ten years ago, you had an employee here, Marilyn De Beer. Her disappearance is now a murder investigation.' Liz let it sink in and watched Robert closely. He didn't flinch. Did he know her? Did he care she was dead? 'We believe, based on our enquiries that Marilyn found something within one of her client's files that likely led to her death.'

'I can't breech client confidentiality without a warrant.'

'True, but if I was to suggest that the client has something to do with the diamond trade, maybe you could do a search through her files for me and point me in the right direction?'

'All your accounts?' Robert tapped his lip with his index finger.

'All my work! Estimated value I'd say thirty-five thousand a year.' His eyebrows rose, the tapping stopped.

'I'll pull her files. See who might be a likely candidate. I'm not promising anything.'

'Neither am I.'

15

'Nice place.' Heather kicked the raised concrete on the path with her Doc Martins that miraculously managed to survive their brush with bitumen.

'Put a sock in it.' Max opened the screen door and put his key in the lock. 'I'm looking at a new place now.'

'Maybe consider a new haircut and a decent shirt label while you're at it.'

'I'm a PI, not an insurance assessor.' The door opened and the musty smell of old carpet and long dead pizza filled his nostrils. *Hell, he didn't do visitors often.*

'Oh, that's foul.' Heather held her nose. 'Who died in here?'

'I'll open up the sliding door. It will air out.' Max threw his keys on the worn out Laminex countertop and took the short walk to the other side of his living room. The sliding door opened with a screech, the rollers almost seized from lack of use.

'Is this a one bedder?' Heather turned slowly around, taking in the torn vinyl stools, the antique kitchen dresser that crammed the living room, so that only two lounge chairs could squeeze into the space.

'Yes.'

'Where am I sleeping?'

'In the recliner.' Max pointed to one of two tan leather grandpa style recliner chairs, complete with little towels to stop hair oil staining the headrest.

'No way.' She moved to leave, but Max stepped into the doorway to stop her.

'Look, someone ransacked your house, then they tried to grab you from the street in broad daylight. You've really put the wind up someone's arse, so best keep a low profile. Hey?'

'I have a case to investigate.'

'No, *we* have a case to investigate. Plus, you've still got mild concussion and the doctor said you need to avoid getting another knock on the head, so I'm here to make sure that doesn't happen.'

Heather touched the recliner as though it might bite. Inspecting it, she decided it was safe and plonked herself down. Leaning back, she popped the foot rest out, pulled out her mobile and promptly flicked off a text message.

'I hope you're not giving anyone this address.' Max opened the fridge and closed it quickly. The smell of sour milk and beer filled the room. He glanced over his shoulder to see if Heather had noticed. Her nose was stuck in her phone.

He'd been on a health kick, but for the most part, he'd been buying his food—takeaway. Sumo Salads, Subway, Thai with lots of vegies, that kind of thing. He hadn't been expecting a house guest. He could only hope they wrapped this up quickly so Heather could go back to her big empty house.

He considered asking her about her family, but decided long, meaningful talks weren't exactly his strong suit.

He grabbed a garbage bag out from under the sink, opened the fridge and swept everything into it, closing both the fridge and the bag as quickly as possible to trap the smells inside.

'Oh my god that's awful.' Heather looked up from her phone. 'I'm going out the back.' She stood and moved to the sliding door. 'What the hell is this for?' Max looked up as he tied the garbage bag closed with a zip tie.

'What?' He watched where she was pointing. 'It's a fly screen.'

'I can't see it keeping flies out with this.' She poked her finger through a large hole by the handle. 'Or a burglar for that matter.'

'It's not as fancy as your place, but it's all I've got.' Max pouted and Heather watched him closely as he stomped out of the front door to the bins at the rear of the parking lot.

He reached the bin, opened the lid and dropped the offending mess in as his mobile rang. Wiping his hands on his jeans, he pulled the phone from his back pocket and hit the answer button.

'Jack, what's up?'

'Just got a report on who Heather's friend is, from the warehouse.'

'I'm listening.' Max moved slowly back to the unit, not wanting to be overheard.

'Turns out Heather's friend is a well-known hacker named Jeremy Marshall.' Max whistled. 'Seems our Youtuber knows people and judging by how jittery she was about me sending a uniform over to his place, he was searching for something for her.'

'What's your plan?'

'Meeting at my place tonight. Anderson, Williams, Liz and you two. We'll see if we can rattle her cage a little. We'll see if the uniform team finds the guy home. Then I'm getting our IT team to see if they can track his online activity.'

'Pretty unlikely. Liz's IT guy Scott might have more luck.'

'Good point. He tends to play in the grey area from what Liz has told me. I'll ask her and see what she can do. In the meantime, keep an eye on Heather.'

'Will do. What time at yours?'

'Six.'

'Six it is.'

16

Liz circled around Jack's small kitchen counter, a wine in one hand, a beer in the other as she made her way out onto the deck overlooking the ocean. The worn timber railing of the seventies built flat was easily ignored against the backdrop of seagulls and setting sun.

'Thanks.' Jack reached for the beer, his fingers lingering on hers a moment. She thought he might kiss her, but when he didn't, she wasn't too concerned.

It was early days and Liz had no idea how regular relationships evolved anymore. Usually, she got paid, slept with her clients, occasionally received a gift or two, then went on to the next client. They either got back to her, or they didn't.

When Jack picked her up for this evening's meeting, she'd watched his body language carefully. He was guarded, and she couldn't blame him for that, but she couldn't help being a little bothered by it either.

'How was Heather?' Liz sipped her wine, regarding Jack as he stared out over the lowering sun.

'She's alive. Her concussion is minor and she went back to Max's place to make sure no one else tries to grab her off the street.' He touched his beer to his lips and Liz could see a question hung unasked.

'I saw Richard Glover today.' He looked at her with a mix of needing to know and not wanting to.

'He was helpful.' Liz kept her tone neutral, wondering if Jack really trusted her yet or not.

'Did he offer to expedite a warrant?'

'I'm persuasive, but even I can't perform miracles.' She wasn't giving him anything. He was going to have to ask or just trust her.

Jack put his beer down on the outdoor table and moved toward her. Taking her wine from her hand, he placed it alongside his beer. When his eyes met hers, she could feel his anguish, but to her surprise, he moved even closer, brushing her cheek with his finger, before holding her chin between thumb and forefinger.

'You're enjoying torturing me with just enough information, way too much.' He brushed his lips on hers and she stifled a shiver.

'I offered him my accounts.' Her voice sounded husky to her ears. She stared at his slightly open lips, and tried not to be too eager. She failed, licking her lips reflexively.

'And what did he say?' Jack moved her back against the balcony railing, his hands either side of her, his voice as rough as hers.

She opened her mouth to answer, but he stopped her with his kiss—soft and seductive at first, then hungry and desperate. Liz wrapped her arms around his neck as he put his hands around her waist, holding her to him.

'Hey. Door was open.' Jenny's voice made them jump apart like school kids caught making out behind the sports shed.

'Out here. Grab yourself a beer.' Jack grinned as Liz straightened her blouse, which he'd pulled out of her pants without her even noticing.

Jenny slid back the curtain, opened the sliding door wider and joined them on the balcony. 'Gorgeous sunset.' She looked at them, a puzzled expression crossed her face but she said nothing.

'Hemi on his way?' Liz picked up her wine.

'He won't be long.'

'The last thing I want to do is hang out with a heap of cops.' Heather's voice was hard to miss, her tone a mixture of anger and frustration.

'You're not hanging out, you're helping out in a police investigation and getting protection for free. We can do it down the station if you prefer?'

'You're not a cop anymore.' They entered the kitchen as Jack, Jenny and Liz left the balcony for the living area.

'No, he isn't, but I am.' Jack finished his beer and moved to the fridge to get another. 'You're here at my request and I thought my place was a little less formal than Headquarters, but we can relocate if you prefer.' He lifted a spare beer from the fridge and offered it to Max.

'You have no idea how much I need this,' Max whispered as he unscrewed the top and took a long, desperate swig.

'I think I can guess.' Jack frowned at Heather. 'Would you like something?'

'Since I'm forced to endure, I guess I might as well.'

'Beer or wine?'

'What beer?'

'Coopers Ale.'

'Shit no. I'll go wine thanks.' Jack moved to the fridge and just as he began to pour, Hemi arrived.

'Kia Ora crew.' The big Maori wore a short-sleeved white tee-shirt, exposing the intricate tribal tattoos that made him look more like a crook than a cop.

'Hey, Anderson, want a wine?' Jack held up the bottle, a spare glass already in his hand.

'That would be choice bro.'

'I'm going to start with the most important update guys.' Jack moved to the round table and Liz became aware that they weren't all going to fit. She moved to Jack's counter and grabbed a stool, Hemi did the same, moving his alongside Jenny.

'Heather, I sent a uniformed unit to your friend's place, Marshall.'

'I told you not to.' She looked like a scared rabbit, surrounded by hungry wolves as Hemi sat down, but as the Kiwi grinned at her, she visibly relaxed.

'You did, but luckily you don't run the show. For someone who investigates cold cases of murder, you're pretty naïve.'

'Compliments will get you everywhere.' The Goth eyeliner was back, along with the attitude.

'Is there anywhere Marshall would hide out if he were in trouble?' Her already pale skin went ghostly white.

'Why? Where is he?'

'He wasn't there, nothing unusual, except, like your place, his was also tossed about. Nothing was left unscathed.'

'Shit!' The fleeting rabbit eyes returned.

'Do you know where Marshall would go?'

Liz watched Heather's leg begin to jostle as she bit down on her thumbnail, the chipped black enamel saying it wasn't the first time.

'I don't know where he'd go. You need to find him.' Her voice shook as she fidgeted, growing more anxious.

'What were they looking for Heather?' Liz touched her hand compassionately. 'I know this is all scary, a bit more than you signed up for when tracking down a cold case, I'm sure, but you have something they want, whether you know it or not.

'Marshall was hacking *Guild and Glover* for me.' She spat the words out.

'Why?' Liz was surprised at Jack's calm tone.

'According to Taiwo, Marilyn had contacted her to find out why one of her clients would have paid her parents' resort, money.'

'You told us that.'

'Yes, but Marilyn called again to say other accounts, not her clients, had also made payments to the *De Beer Game Reserve* in Botswana.'

'Okay, so you had Marshall hacking to find out who all the clients were?' Liz waited for a reply. Heather nodded, her thumbnail back between her teeth.

'That doesn't explain what you have that someone else wants.' Max joined the interrogation, causing Heather to look from Jack, to Liz, to Max, then Hemi, with his big arms and bikie tattoos, his grin suddenly not enough to put her at ease.

Liz saw the wall come up. Heather moved her chair back. 'I need to find Marshall.'

'No, *we* need to find him. You need to tell us everything you know before someone else ends up dead.'

'I can't.'

'Heather. Who are you protecting? What have you got that someone wants so badly?' Liz tried to keep her tone calm but the girl's expression made everyone nervous.

'Hey team. This is getting us nowhere.' Jenny sat the other side of Hemi and had remained silent until now. 'We've already got everyone out looking for Marshall. We'll start on it ourselves tomorrow. Let's just take a chill pill, grab some pizza and recap on what we *do* know.'

Everyone looked at Jenny a moment, before Max grinned. 'Good idea Williams. I'm always happy to drink another beer and if someone else is paying for the pizza, I'm in.' Liz chuckled, Heather let out a breath she'd been holding and Jack sat back, arms crossed, but his expression said he wasn't going to push Heather, not just yet anyway.

'I'll order the pizza.' Liz offered, bringing up the pizza app on her phone. It was always safer to do the ordering when you were the gluten free eater.

'I'll have anything vegetarian.' Hemi looked hungry as Liz showed him the menu options.

'I'll go the pepperoni.' Jack took a slow, calming breath.

Max made to open his mouth, but Liz interrupted. 'I've already ordered you the meat lovers.'

'You know me so well.' He got up to get more beer.

'What's with you two,' Heather looked from Max to Liz, then from Liz to Jack, 'and you two?'

Liz stopped tapping the order out on the pizza app a moment, her fingers hovering over the screen as she looked from Max to Jack.

'I'm her ex-husband, now business partner. Jack is my ex-partner from my cop days.'

'That explains you two, but what about you two?' She pointed to Jack and Liz.

'We are friends.' Jack answered a little too quickly. 'Like we told you, we work together on cases from time to time.'

'What pizza do you want Heather?' Liz decided that changing the conversation direction was easier than explaining her relationship with Jack. Hell, if they didn't know what their relationship was, no one else was going to figure it out.

17

'I can give you a lift home if you like Liz, I'm not far from you.' Jenny stood at the door ready to leave, Hemi waiting by her side.

'Thanks, but I think you have other matters to attend to.' She nodded toward the big Kiwi. 'Jack and I have more to go over anyway.' She wasn't about to explain what *more* entailed.

She shut the door, turned and leant against it, slowly taking a deep breath. Max and Heather had left a few minutes before, arguing like father and daughter before they reached the end of the balcony.

'I thought they'd never leave.' Jack moved toward her, her back still against the door. Leaning in, he kissed her softly. 'Where were we when we were rudely interrupted earlier?' His warm breath next to her ear made her skin tingle and her stomach flutter, something she hadn't felt since high school.

'I'd just told you I hadn't been persuasive enough to convince Richard Glover to give you free rein and willingly approve a warrant to search his records.' Jack pulled back. 'But I did convince him to search Marilyn's files himself and if something jumped out, he'd let me know.'

'I always knew you were very persuasive.' Jack put his arm around her waist and pulled her to him.

'What can I persuade *you* to do Detective?' Liz pushed away from the door, bringing Jack along with her as she pulled his marble grey tee-shirt off over his head, revealing a tanned, trim torso.

'Just about anything you want.' He lifted her from her feet, hands wrapped tightly over her backside, gripping her as she wrapped her legs around his waist and flung her arms around his neck, devouring his lips.

'Do you think they know?' Liz asked breathlessly between locking lips and pulling away to unbutton her blouse.

'I think they have an inkling, but it's fun making them wonder.' Jack carried her down the hall to his room.

She squealed as he tossed her down gently on the bed, watching her from a distance, not moving to join her. She patted the space next to her, but he remained standing, scanning her, his expression voyeuristic, his eyes dark with excitement.

'You sure you want this?'

She shimmied back to lean against the headboard. 'Want you to take off your pants and have a repeat of last night?' She scoffed at the dumbness of the question. 'Why the hell wouldn't I want that?'

He sat down next to her, his movements slow, careful, precise. 'That's not want I meant. We both want the sex, we both need the connection, but are you really sure you want me—long term because I don't do casual.'

Liz knelt up on her knees, moving down the bed to the end where he sat, motionless, holding his breath for the answer. She stood, undid her pants and let them fall to the floor, revealing a simple black G-string that matched her very basic black bra.

Wearing her former professional underwear around Jack had seemed wrong, and she'd worried he might think about *Foxy* if she had.

Now, as his eyes followed the curves of her body, she wondered if it would have mattered, but the choice had been strategic, to make the answer to his question clear. Yet he was still asking it.

She moved back to the bed, pushing him flat on his back as she straddled his hips. 'Understand one thing very clearly Mr

Cunningham.' His eyebrows rose. She'd never called him by his last name. Always Detective, or Jack. 'I gave up my past for you. *You!* How can you even ask me that question?' She pouted deliberately.

Jack was silent a moment, as though he were carefully gathering his thoughts before answering her question. 'You said you'd given up, but we haven't really talked about it.'

'Talking is over-rated.' Liz pinned his hands by his head and leant down to brush her lips against his, trying anything to avoid the conversation she knew had to be had.

'Liz.' She stopped kissing him, pulling back at the tone in his voice. 'You know I love you.' She smiled. 'But I don't want your past coming back to bite us.'

She rolled from on top of him, throwing herself into the soft pillow and quilt, her face flooded with emotion. 'You're ashamed of what I've done.'

'No!' He rolled over and stared into her eyes, stroking her cheek with his fingers, she turned away, not wanting him to see the tears that were threatening to slide free. 'Absolutely not.'

'What then? I don't understand. I'm not working anymore. I've cut off all my past clients. What more is there to talk about?' Her emotions were reeling. This was exactly what she'd been afraid of all this time—the reason she'd never made a move on Jack and waited for him to take the lead.

Jack took her head gently by the chin and turned her to face him, his eyes begging her to understand. 'You still own a brothel Liz and I'm a Senior Major Crimes Detective, we can't exactly come out in the open and tell the world.' His lips were so close. Liz wanted to kiss him with every fibre of her being, but what was he saying?

'What you're really asking is do *you* want this, not me?' Liz shook herself free of his touch. 'You let me know when you've decided.' She got off the bed and looked for her clothes, picking up her pants first. Jack reached for her, but she pulled back.

'I'll take a taxi home. I'll talk to you tomorrow about Marilyn's case.'

'Liz!' Jack moved toward her, she put her hand up, palm first to stop him.

'*You* need to decide what's more important Jack. Me or your reputation.' She left the bedroom.

'Liz.' He jumped up and followed her down the hallway. 'You've got this all wrong.'

'No, you have Jack. Us, you and me—we both have baggage, lots of it.'

'Exactly. I want to talk it through. How we manage it, publicly.'

'I'm not ready to talk Jack.' She picked up her bag and pulled out her phone to call a taxi. 'I just wanted a few days, months,' she shook her head. 'I don't know, maybe even years— where my past didn't ruin my present.'

'Liz.'

She moved to the door, stopped with it half open and looked at his face. She could see he was torn, but so was she. She knew he was a detective and she was a Madam and it was beyond complicated. She knew he was borderline OCD and should have realised that floating around without clear boundaries was going to freak him out, but right now all she'd wanted was to forget for a minute.

'I'll see you tomorrow Jack. Let's just focus on the case for now.' She closed the door and took a long, slow breath before she moved toward the stairs. Part of her wanted him to open the door and chase after her, but the other part hoped he wouldn't.

18

Jack reached out to turn off his alarm, before realising it was his phone that had woken him. He answered, 'Detective Cunningham.'

He listened, rubbing his eyes to try and remove the sleep and get them to focus. 'Has Williams been called?'

'Okay. I'll be there in thirty minutes.' Jack rolled over. A sigh left his lips as he touched the vacant space next to him. It had been too many years since he'd shared his bed with a woman. Now he'd broken the ice with Liz he was afraid it would ruin everything. He wondered if he should never have told her how he felt.

Shaking himself free of his foul mood, he got up and headed for a quick cold shower to wake himself up properly.

Ten minutes later he was in his car on his way to the call out. He pressed *call* on his Bluetooth hands-free unit that was strapped to the back of his sun visor, once again wondering why he hadn't parted with his old car or upgraded to a new smart phone. *Was he so stuck in the past?*

'I'm on scene Boss.' Williams answered before Jack could ask a question.

'Good, I'm five minutes out.'

'It's Marshall, I've confirmed his prints from his police record.'

'Long rap sheet then?'

'He's been caught hacking into government databases. An agenda in social justice issues seems to be his key motive, but income shouldn't be ruled out.'

'So blood diamonds and funding civil war could be right up his alley.'

'I'd say so.'

'The only question is, was it for activism or profit? Okay, secure the scene, get the uniforms canvasing the area and I'll be there in a minute.'

'Will do.'

Jack let the call drop out as Williams hung up, his mind racing over how Heather even knew Marshall and why he'd agreed to hack in to *Guild and Glover* for her. Was it the hacking that got him killed, or was it diamonds and what was the connection to the De Beer family in South Africa?

His old BMW bottomed out on the speed bump as he drove into the abandoned carpark of the soon to be demolished commercial shopping centre on Main South Road. The overpass and new roads had left the area rundown and disused. Jack couldn't help but wonder what they were going to turn the place into.

Williams met him as he opened the door to get out. 'The complex is due for demolition next week.'

'Who found the body?' Jack walked with Williams as she led the way.

'The Site Manager. Came out this morning to do a final recon before scheduling the excavators and dump trucks for Monday.'

'So Marshall could have been buried in rubble and picked up with the rubbish?'

'Looks like it. Someone didn't want him to be found. Penny is on scene already. Maybe she can give you a little more detail. I'll finish up interviewing the manager so he can leave.'

'Good idea.' Jack took the gloves Jenny offered him and smiled. 'Thanks'

'All part of the job Boss.' She returned the smile as she moved away to finish her work. Jack took a deep breath and moved to join the forensic investigator, thankful it was Penny on site. The scientist was thorough and always quick to follow up on major cases like this.

'What you got?'

'Doc Holbrook is on his way Jack. I'll let him give you a run down on cause of death and possible window, but this scene is really interesting.'

'In what way?' Jack put on a pair of shoe covers before moving in to examine the victim.

'Well, this for one thing.' Penny pointed to a folder on the ground, a footprint clearly visible on the surface next to evidence marker number three.

'What size do you think it is?'

'I don't know yet, probably a UK ten, but that isn't the interesting part.' Penny moved forward, a stainless-steel implement in her hand that looked like a pen, but wasn't. As she flipped the folder open, Jack realised what she was talking about.

Inside were various photos of diamonds. Penny moved them with her pointer, being careful not to damage anything. Every photo was printed in black and white, featuring velvet bags with cut and uncut diamonds likely worth millions.

'Why would a digital hacker have physical photos on him?' Penny looked up to Jack's question, a frown forming between her brows.

'I don't think this is his folder.'

'The killer dropped it? That would be sloppy.'

'I agree. That's your job to figure that out. Mine is to match prints.' She flipped the folder closed once more. 'Including boot prints.'

'Let's hope we find a boot to match it with. You should head over to Marshall's place when you finish here. See if you can find any boots in his closet that match. He looks like he could be a size ten.'

'Will do.'

'Penny.' The scientist looked up from her camera as she snapped more photos of the scene.

'Yep.'

'We've got two dead bodies now. This isn't a cold case anymore.'

'I'll put a rush on it Jack. As best I can. We're a little snowed under but I'll do my best.' Penny nodded behind Jack. 'Here comes Doc.'

'Hey Doc. How's your morning been?' Jack turned to welcome the pathologist and chief medical officer who always looked like a quintessential mortician with his wild grey hair and dark circles around his eyes.

'It started pleasantly, then this.' The pathologist had been in the job as long as Jack had been a detective and he often wondered just how much death the doctor had been witness to.

'I'll come back in a minute and see what you've got for me.' Jack moved past the doctor to join Williams who was finishing up her interview with the site manager.

'Williams,' he called. 'I've just got a few questions.' Jenny nodded and the site manager shifted his weight from one foot to the other.

'Who else would have known you were bringing this place down Monday?' Jack swept his arm around the disused site, noticing the faded signs and boarded up windows and wondering if progress was really a good thing when all this building material would be heading to landfill and another load of construction would take its place.

'The excavation company—they've been on standby for this job for a week, then there's my boss at the firm, a few site workers who will be handling safety. I told your off-sider here already.'

'I'm getting a list Sir.' Jenny kept procedure formal and Jack nodded.

'So the list isn't huge, but you're not the only person to know already that Monday is demo day?'

'Well it isn't now.'

The site manager looked at his feet, chewed his lip, then tried to make eye contact. 'I wasn't the first to know.'

'Who was?'

'My boss. He called me last night, after hours, bugging me about the ETA on demo for this site.'

'Is that usual?' Jack looked at Jenny whose eyebrows were asking the same question he was thinking.

'Not unheard of mate, but not usual, no.'

'You can go now, but I want that list of all employees and companies involved by four PM today and I need your boss's name now.'

'George Baxter is my boss.' The manager rubbed his left shoulder before putting both hands in his pockets.

'Give Detective Williams the details, phone number, address, company position, then you can leave.' Jack nodded for Jenny to take the details. 'I'll check in with the Doc.'

19

Jack stared at his desk computer screen, not seeing anything, his mind churning over Liz, Marilyn, the hacker kid's dead eyes, and the folder of diamond photos.

'Coffee's up.' Jenny put the latte down on the desk, pushing it under Jack's nose to bring him back to the real world.

'Thanks.' He reached down, lifted the reusable mug to his lips and savoured the flavour, letting the caffeine do its job. 'I needed that.'

'You looked like you did.' Jenny took a sip of her own coffee which Jack knew would have contained an extra kick of caramel syrup. 'Have you told Max to let Heather know yet?'

'He hasn't told her, but he's bringing her in.'

'Liz on her way?'

'I haven't called her.' Jenny looked at him a moment, before obviously deciding it wasn't the right time to push him.

'So we have a cold case, that is now a new murder investigation.'

'That's what the Doc says, at least his preliminary exam does. We'll need to wait for the full report before we know for sure, but Doc Holbrook said the cause of death looks a lot like Marilyn's. Blunt force trauma to the head.'

'He didn't just trip out there and hit his head on the concrete?'

'Doc reckons there is a wound pattern that might reveal more, but the location of the body and the head injury are not consistent with a fall.'

'So what did Marshall stumble upon that got him killed and who owns the folder of diamond photos?'

'Diamond photos?' Jack turned at the sound of Liz's voice. 'You know I found diamond ring photos in Marilyn's possessions.'

He watched her walk in like she belonged in the Major Crimes office and grinned at the thought, recalling their first interview when Becca's body had been found and Liz had come in to identify her. She'd been distraught at the time, but still able to nail his arse to the wall when he tried to fob her off and send her home to wait on his investigation. Now, here they were, working together. He'd never have picked it.

'Max called you.' Jenny stated the obvious.

'He did.' She looked pointedly at Jack, who averted his eyes. 'He's bringing Heather down, but I'm not sure what we'll get out of her. She's going to be petrified now Marshall is dead.'

Jack took a deep breath and pulled himself together. 'I agree.'

'What was that about diamond photos, in Marilyn's possessions?' Jenny watched them both carefully, reading the temperature in the room as she waited for an answer.

'When Jack dropped Marilyn's gear off at my place, I found photos of diamond rings in a folder, taken out of magazines. I thought maybe she was just engagement ring hunting, but Jack said they hadn't discussed getting married.' She looked at him, but Jack struggled to read the motive behind the words.

'So you think they are connected?' Jenny pushed.

'I'm sure they are.' She put a folder on his desk and opened it up, showing the various rings. 'These are all magazine ads for three major jewellery stores. All in Adelaide.'

'Diamonds seem the likely link Williams.' Jack backed Liz up. 'Heather said Taiwo was talking to Marilyn about diamond verification, and Liz showed me the magazine clippings of diamonds in Marilyn's personal effects. But now we have the diamond photos on the scene of Marshall's murder, we have to assume diamonds are involved.'

'They must be the link.' Liz assured them both. 'Robert Glover called me this morning.' Jack waited for her to continue. 'He did a little digging and this jeweller,' she pointed to a pink diamond and white gold ring featured on an elegantly long fingered hand model with impeccable pale pink nails, 'was Marilyn's client. It wasn't until he mentioned the name that I recalled these pictures.'

'That makes sense, but what about the other two jewellers?' Jenny picked up the magazine article, admiring the ring and Jack smiled knowingly. Liz met his eyes and grinned to acknowledge she could see the ring envy in the young detective's eyes.

'Robert said unofficially, that they were both clients of his firm, but Marilyn didn't handle their accounts.'

'That fits with what Heather said about Marilyn asking Taiwo about more clients of the firm, but we don't know if they were all jewellers, only that they all paid money to Marilyn's parents' game reserve in South Africa.'

'Then we start digging into these three jewellers and what could link them with Marilyn's parents.' Jack picked up his cup and finished his coffee, sighing that they might finally be getting somewhere with the case.

'We still need to tell Heather that Marshall is dead.' Jenny brought him back to earth.

'And we need to interview the site manager's boss. There's a link we are missing—I can feel it in my gut.'

'There is also Marilyn's parents' game reserve connection. You said Hemi gave you the dates the De Beers visited Australia. Do you have those dates?' Liz sat on the edge of Jack's desk. He resisted the urge to reach for her hand.

Instead, he focussed on his partner who looked from him to Liz questioningly.

She finally answered. 'Yes. I'll bring them up now.' She plucked away at the keys and tapped her finger on the mouse as she waited for the files to appear.

'She and Hemi make a cute couple, don't you think?' Liz was looking at Jenny as she spoke. The young detective was deliberately not paying her any attention.

'They do.' He pushed his empty mug to the side of his desk, annoyed he was fidgeting like a school boy. Taking a deep breath, he started to speak just as Liz did.

'I'm sorry I took off.'

'I'm sorry I opened...' They laughed and Jack continued, 'my big mouth.' Jack saw Jenny look sideways, but return her attention to the screen quickly.

Liz put her hand on his and squeezed. 'I'm out of practice.'

'That makes two of us.'

'Okay.' Jenny looked up, her eyes lingering on their hands as Jack put his back in his lap and Liz did the same. The younger detective grinned. 'Mr and Mrs De Beer's last visit to Australia was in June, twenty-o-nine.'

'Shit!'

'What!' Jenny and Liz turned to ask simultaneously.

'That's the same month Marilyn left.'

'And a week later, she was dead,' Liz clarified.

20

Jenny started tapping on her keyboard once again, frantically looking up the case notes. 'Your statement says you last saw Marilyn on the morning of June ten, when you left early for work and she was still in bed.'

'I know what's in the report Williams.' Jack tried not to sound as frustrated as he felt.

'You do, but Liz doesn't.'

'What doesn't she know?' Max walked into the office, Heather by his side. Seconds later, the Chief appeared, Bridges in hot pursuit.

'What is this place, Adelaide Railway Station?' He looked from Liz to Max, then back to Jack who swallowed hard, waiting for the onslaught.

'Just chasing up leads in that cold case Sir.'

'Which looks like it's linked to our new case Sir.' Jenny backed Jack up, looking carefully at Heather.

'Bridges said you'd brought in your own consultants Jack. I said I'd get you the extra manpower if you needed it.'

'I'm aware of that Sir and thank you, but the division has enough on their plate and Ms Jeffreys and Max offered their services.'

'There's no budget for consultants Cunningham.' Liz stood up, walked over to the Chief and tapped him gently on the forearm. Jack cringed when he saw the lust in the Chief's eyes. Liz and he had history and the thought made Jack's stomach roll, but he took a deep breath and reminded himself that they both had a past and more baggage to go with it than anyone cared to consider good.

'Chief, I'm not charging. This is the least I could do to help Detective Cunningham out after he solved Becca's murder and you can't expect Max to sit by and do nothing when his former partner is in need, now can you?' He wasn't an expert, but Liz's body language said she still knew how to wrap a guy around her finger. He couldn't help but wonder if he was just another guy to be manipulated.

He shook the thought aside. She'd never tried a move like that on him. In fact, that was why it had taken him so long to do anything about their relationship—whatever their relationship was. He hadn't been sure how he felt, but more importantly, he hadn't been sure how she felt either.

'Well, I guess we can't turn down extra help when it's free of charge.' He winked and Liz patted his hand. Max chuckled and shook his head.

'Will someone tell me what the hell is going on here?' Heather looked from Max to Liz and the Chief, then on past them to Jack. 'Why am I even here?'

'You're here because someone has tossed your place and then tried to kidnap you.' Jack waggled his finger and the Chief gave a casual salute to excuse himself. 'And because we have some bad news.' Jack allowed his tone to soften, knowing the next few words were going to scare the living daylights out of the young self-appointed private investigator, come investigative journalist as she like to call herself.

'Why don't you take a seat.' Liz offered.

'I don't need a bloody seat. I need to know what's going on!'

'We've found Marshall, but...'

'He's dead isn't he?' Max pulled a chair out from Bridges' desk in time for Heather to plonk down heavily next to Jack's desk.

'What makes you say that?' Jack turned his chair to face her, as she placed her hands in her lap, picking at her nail varnish habitually.

'I told him it was dangerous.'

'What was dangerous Heather?' Jack noticed Bridges' ears prick up as he sat at his own desk, trying to pretend like he wasn't eavesdropping.

'He wanted to help me.' Jack watched as her eyeliner began to run with the tears down her face. He held his hand out, and Liz passed him a box of tissues from Jenny's desk. Her eyes met his and spoke volumes.

Heather took the offered tissue and covered her eyes with it, somehow hoping to block out the pain. Jack didn't push. Instead, he waited, as all eyes were on the girl with the attitude, who'd lost her parents young and spent the last few years trying to solve old murders in the hopes of discovering why her own parents had died.

'I didn't tell him everything,' she sniffed. 'But he said he could hack into the *Guild and Glover* database and find out who the other clients were that Marilyn was talking about.' Jack waited, nodding to Williams to take notes.

'We knew diamonds were involved or Marilyn wouldn't have mentioned the extra clients to Taiwo. It made sense they'd be jewellers or diamond importers.' Jack forced himself not to interrupt, but if she'd known all along that the other clients Marilyn talked about had been jewellers, she could have saved them a lot of work and maybe Marshall's life. He looked at Liz whose expression said what he was thinking. He gently shook his head. She wasn't one to mince words and now wasn't the time to get Heather offside.

'Okay, we know you asked Marshall to find out which other clients of *Guild and Glover* Marilyn was interested in.' She nodded. 'But you knew it was dangerous, you said so yourself.' His tone was quiet, gentle.

'He didn't just hack *Guild and Glover*.' The sniffing turning into sobbing. 'I shouldn't have told him about the recording.' Jack looked at Max who shrugged to say he had no idea what she was talking about.

'What recording Heather?' Jack saw Bridges move closer, discretion giving way to curiosity. He still didn't know if he wanted Bridges in on this case. The guy was new, ex-Sydney, either a whistle blower or a dirty cop and he'd just been brown nosing with the Chief, spilling the beans about Max and Liz consulting on the case. Was he trustworthy?

'Taiwo.'

'What about Taiwo.' Jack felt his frustration rising. They'd still not been able to get anyone to find Taiwo in Botswana let alone interview her and they really needed to contact Marilyn's parents. There never seemed to be enough hours in the day.

'I recorded our last conversation.' She pulled another tissue from the box. 'I told him what Taiwo said.'

'What did she say Heather? Where is the recording?' Jack's patience was wearing thin now. 'People are dying Heather. Marshall is dead. Where is the recording?'

'I can't get her to answer my calls. I've tried.'

'Give us the recording Heather and no one will have any reason to chase you anymore. We'll handle it. We'll find Taiwo.'

'It was going to be my big Youtube exposé. My chance to be taken seriously.'

'Heather.' Liz moved around in front of the young woman and lowered herself to her haunches so they were at eye level. 'I left home at about the same age you lost your parents. I know you've had it tough and this murder story might have been your big ticket to getting your parents' case reopened, but you're right in the mix now. I'll investigate your parents' death, but you need to help Jack and his team out now. Where is the recording?'

Heather wiped her tears, the tissue covered in black eye makeup dropped to the ground from her lap as she reached inside her black shirt.

The room was dead quiet as she retrieved a necklace, taking the chain over her head and holding the locket in her hand a moment before making eye contact with Jack. 'This might help catch Marshall's killer.'

She passed the gold, intricately carved pendant to Jack, who took it, his thoughts confused as he studied it.

'Open it,' she instructed. He did. Inside was a micro-SD card, the type used in most mobile phones and many cameras or recording devices. 'It's not enough to incriminate any one person, but it was probably what got Marshall killed. They were likely looking for this.'

Jack handed the locket to Williams, who retrieved a glove from her jacket pocket and put it on before he dropped the SD card out into her palm. Not that there would be any evidence on it, but he didn't want to risk damaging the card and making the contents illegible.

'Why do you think this got Marshall killed?'

'Because the De Beers are tied up in this. That recording is Taiwo telling me she had proof, but she disappeared. So Marshall tried to hack into her company's computers. That was just before my place was ransacked.'

'Why the hell didn't you tell us all this when we investigated your break in?' Jack's patience evaporated. No Goth tears were going to stop him now. 'I don't understand Heather. Why?'

'Because this case was what she needed to get her parents' case re-opened.' Liz offered a reply. 'The criminal system works for some Jack, but not all of us.' Jack knew very little about Liz's family issues. He knew her dad had died of natural causes and she was estranged from her mother, but what case did she feel hadn't been dealt with properly?

'I'll tell you about it sometime.' Liz answered his unasked question. 'For now, let's listen to that recording.' She nodded to the SD card.

'You're right.' He patted Heather's hand. 'We can't bring Marshall back, or Marilyn or your parents, but we'll do what we can to solve their deaths.' She looked at him, suddenly looking more vulnerable than he thought possible. 'I'll start digging into your parents' case with Liz until we find something, anything that can get it reopened, but no more secrets. Deal?'

Her eyes drilled into his for long enough that he had to fight the urge to look away. 'Deal.'

21

'Okay, you take Heather home Max, we'll…'

'No way. You can't shut me out just like that.' Heather stood, her tears forgotten as her hands made their way to her hips indignantly.

'I can.'

'Jack.' Liz intervened. 'She's right. Her friend is dead, just like Marilyn. You both have a vested interest in this case.'

'Yes, but we aren't both Senior Detectives.' He looked to Williams for support but she was busy loading the micro SD card carefully into an adapter.

'We can argue all day or we can go listen to that recording and make a plan for catching a killer, or two.' Liz's hands mirrored Heather's now.

'Don't fight it mate. Pick your battles.' Max grinned as he lounged back against his old desk next to Williams in a chair he'd retrieved from the still vacant desk that was once Johnnie's, before Williams had been forced to shoot him dead.

Bridges studied the murder board that stood on rollers between his desk and Jack's side of the room. 'Looks like this needs updating. Do you need a hand?'

'Why not?' Jack's tone was defeated. 'After we all listen to the recording I guess.' Liz watched him take a long, slow breath before puffing out his cheeks with the exhale.

Jenny stood, waved the SD card in the adapter and turned to leave the room. 'I need to copy this securely before we listen, so follow me to Ops if you want to hear what's on it.'

Liz stood back and watched as the trail of interested parties followed the auburn haired, tall and lean young detective out into the hallway and down toward the operations room. Jack stopped at the doorway and turned around, lingering.

'You coming?' He finally spoke.

'Sure.' She moved toward him.

He frowned as she approached. 'What are you grinning at?'

'You.' She drew closer. He waited. 'You want to kiss and make up later? Or are you too frustrated and upset still?' She slapped him on the backside as she moved past into the hallway.

Jack shook his head. 'You and your mini me are turning out to be quite the challenge, but I think I'm up for it.' She chuckled, but didn't look back as he moved to catch up to her.

'When you're ready you two.' Max stood holding the Ops door wide open, a silly grin on his face saying he knew exactly what was going on.

'About time you two sorted your shit out,' he whispered as they moved inside and he let the door close.

'Don't know what you're talking about.' Liz feigned innocence.

'Okay. Give me a second.' Jenny sat in front of a wall of monitors, clicking keys on the lonesome keyboard that occupied the excessively long white melamine desk. The first screen showed the files being copied. She opened the case notes on another screen.

Clicking the mouse over the finished copy, she dragged the file from one screen to the other, dropping it into the case notes and closing them. 'Okay. Ready to roll.' She clicked a few buttons and the audio file opened in a media player on yet another viewing screen.

'Let's hear what's so important that someone wants to kill for it.' She hit the play arrow as everyone fell silent, and a hissing background noise filled the room.

I can't talk to you. They know we've been in contact. It was a mistake to ever contact you. The native South African accent made it obvious to anyone listening it was likely Taiwo's voice.

Marilyn didn't run away like you thought. She's dead Taiwo. Heather.

Don't you think I understand that! Don't call me again. The De Beers are big here, bigger than you can imagine and what they do is backed by the people I work for, and the local authorities.

Who killed Marilyn Taiwo? You must know?

Don't call me again!

The line went dead. No one spoke as the contents of the recording sank in. It was Jack who finally broke the silence.

'Whoever is after you, is after this. Right?'

'I'd guess so.'

'But Taiwo doesn't name anyone except the De Beers.' Jack continued.

'Well, she doesn't name anyone, but she indicates her boss is involved, or at least the company she works for,' Liz added.

'I haven't been able to speak to Taiwo since this call.' Heather looked concerned.

'If she were dead, they wouldn't be chasing this tape.' Liz circled around the room to offer support.

'Not necessarily.' Jack missed Liz's warning to not say what he was thinking out loud. 'If she is already dead, that makes this recording the last missing piece in tying up loose ends.'

'This recording isn't the only loose end.' Max tapped Heather on the shoulder. 'She's still a witness. The only reason they haven't killed her is because of this recording.' Liz rolled her eyes at Max, who missed the exasperation.

Heather searched Liz's face, her eyes showing her fear.

'Agreed.' Jack pulled out his mobile. 'We need to speed up finding someone in Botswana who can find Taiwo and interview the De Beers.'

'You calling Anderson again?' Jenny moved to the back of the room to remove the SD card from the bank of computer equipment.

'I think he's our best bet, but we need to get some answers before someone else winds up dead.' Jack waited as the call rang out to voice mail. 'Anderson, it's Jack, give me a call when you have a minute. Thanks mate.' He hung up, placing his phone back in his pocket.

'You've got a lot of moving parts on this Cunningham.' Bridges spoke and all eyes fell on him, suddenly remembering the ex-Sydney cop was in the room.

'You've got that right. Let's get out of here and update the whiteboard with what we know.' Jack moved toward the door. 'Then we can divide and hopefully conquer.'

22

Liz moved up alongside Jack as they filed out of Ops and made their way back to the Major Crimes office.

'You could call the De Beers you know.' Jack looked at Liz, a question on his lips but she didn't give him time to ask it. 'You were practically their son-in-law and their daughter's body has finally been found.'

'I see where you are going.'

'It's a good idea.' Max joined the conversation, moving up from behind them. 'Suss out their reaction. Ask them why they haven't come out to retrieve her body for burial.'

'Yeah. Why haven't they?' Heather backed Max up. The PI nodded his approval.

Everyone remained silent as they moved back into the office, the sound of a phone ringing in the distance the only noise to break into everyone's thoughts.

Jack picked up a red marker pen, Liz sat on the edge of his desk, Max returned to his chair by his old desk as Bridges pulled a roller chair over from his own. Heather seemed lost for anywhere to perch herself. Instead, she paced the floor like a leopard in a cage.

Jenny was last to arrive, and stood at the back of the room, her arms crossed, her eyes focussed on the whiteboard.

'Okay. We have Marilyn's body—confirmed death by blunt force trauma.' Jack put a star next to the photo of Marilyn's remains, above the photo of the living woman and Liz wondered how he was coping behind his professional mask. Much like her when she had been working, Jack was good at putting on a front.

'We know the De Beers visited Adelaide before Marilyn went missing.' Jack put a line from Marilyn's photo upward, added the word *parents* and the date they arrived.

'That could be coincidence.' Liz offered without any real conviction.

'Except they didn't come to meet Jack, or visit Marilyn at home.' Max tapped his nose. 'That says something is a little off to me.'

'Did they visit her at work maybe?' Jenny joined in with her own speculation.

'Good point. Maybe you can check with her work colleagues Williams?' Jack pointed his red marker at her as he spoke.

'Will do Boss.' The junior detective made a note on her phone, but didn't call right away. Instead, her eyes were quickly fixed back on the board as clues began to mount.

'I have a few people I can check with who might be able to answer that question too,' Liz added.

'Glover?' Jack asked.

'And the receptionist.' Liz could see the cogs turning in Jack's mind, but she wasn't about to tell him the woman had taken her up on the offer to work part-time as an escort.

'Then we have Taiwo, who had been Marilyn's best friend in Botswana. She works for a company that manages ethical diamond certification. Marilyn rings her and quizzes her about why her client is making payments to her parents' resort. Why does she think Taiwo will know anything? We need financial forensics to trace those payments. Do we have any proof that Marilyn's client was paying that money to the De Beers?'

'No, but we know who the client is from Robert Glover.' Liz stood up, moved to the board, retrieved the marker from Jack with a cheeky grin, swayed her way to the board and wrote the name *Elegant and Elite* between Marilyn's photo and the *Ethical Diamond* box. 'We also know the other two clients of *Guild and Glover*, who weren't Marilyn's clients but she was still investigating them.' She added the names *Mills and Burns*, and *The Diamond House* to the board.

'We need to dig up everything we can about the comings and goings of the directors, or managers of these companies.' She handed the marker back to Jack.

'I can do that.' Bridges offered. Jack looked to Max, who gave a slight nod.

'Good, you do the background digging. Have they travelled to Botswana? Do any of them have any financial issues?' Bridges nodded, a sudden look of excitement making his eyes glint.

'I think I might need to look at an engagement ring.' Liz smiled as Jack almost choked on her suggestion, while Max laughed out loud and Jenny sniggered. 'For the case,' she clarified. 'I'll start with *Elegant and Elite* and work my way through them all. Let's see what sort of certification they offer on their stock.'

'Be careful Liz. We've got two dead bodies already.' Jack moved to add Marshall's photo to the whiteboard as he spoke. He put the new photo next to Marilyn's and drew a red line between them with the words *Hacking Guild and Glover* and *Taiwo's firm* along it. 'Do we know who Taiwo works for yet?' He looked to Heather.

'Van der Sandt Exports.'

'Okay, Williams. Let's see if we can find a link between them and the De Beers.' Jack picked up a photo of Heather.

'Hey. Where did you get that?' She frowned. 'I'm not dead, you can't put my photo up there.'

'You are a link in the case. That's all.' Jack assured her. 'You are linked to Marilyn's investigation, Taiwo and Marshall.

Do you have a photo of Taiwo?' Jack asked as he added the photo next to the word *Heather* he'd added earlier. He then wrote the words *YouTuber – Cold Case Digger*.

'No, I don't and I'm not a digger, I'm an investigative journalist.' She took a big breath as she moved up alongside Max, finally stopping her pacing to plant her hands back on her hips.

'We'll see. So far you've just dug yourself into trouble,' Jack smiled, but Heather wasn't taking the comment as it was intended.

'I've solved three unsolved murders you know.' Jack grinned even more widely, but Heather still wasn't backing down.

'He's baiting you.' Max whispered not so quietly from his relaxed position, feet up on his old desk. She gave him a dark eyed look that could melt solid rock, but stopped buying into Jack's taunting.

'Williams. Can you get a photo of Taiwo? We need to pass it on to Botswana authorities in any case.'

'On it.' Jenny added it to her notes. 'What are our theories so far?'

'Marilyn stumbled on transactions between her jeweller client and her parents in Botswana. She'd been estranged from them since moving to Australia. They've visited a number of times, but I don't believe they ever met with her while here—you can confirm that though Williams.' Jenny nodded.

'Taiwo works for a diamond certification company called *Van der Stadt* in Botswana and we have a recording indicating she is scared, that she knows something about a link between her work, the De Beers and Marilyn's death. I think we are talking blood diamonds. Marilyn found out, but before she could tell me or get enough evidence to give me, she was kidnapped and killed.'

'Sounds like a solid theory, now we need to prove it.' Max pushed his chair back and stood abruptly. 'I might know a few people, from the old days.'

Jack and Liz both knew Max had a history of dirty dealings when he was on the force. It had all been innocent enough. Accepting a bribe here, letting a pimp off lightly there. He'd always justified it as making sure he kept his ear to the ground for any real corruption and it would have been fine except he got caught up with Jack's dad, Judge Cunningham, who single-handedly ran the underbelly of Adelaide until Becca's murder.

When Liz had come back into Max's life to find Becca's murderer, all the roads had led to Jack's corrupt dad. When Max realised that the man he worked for could have killed Becca, he'd pulled the pin on the whole operation. Of course, all the big players had walked away clean, but Becca's murderer was now behind bars.

Max had freed himself from the corruption, but it had cost him his badge, something he'd regretted, until Liz had offered him the PI job.

'Tread carefully mate.' Jack nodded as Max moved toward the door.

'Heather. You're still with me.' He waved for her to follow. 'Someone still wants you dead.'

'They might want you all dead if they figure out you've got that recording now.' Heather moved to join Max, seemingly not so resistant as before to go with the rough old PI guy.

'That gives me an idea.' Liz turned from watching Max leaving, to Jack. His eyebrow rose as he saw her expression. A mixture of excitement and anxiety. 'We need to leak out to the press that we have this recording now.' She waited for a response. Max had stopped at the office doorway, Bridges turned in his chair and Jenny had tucked her phone away in her jacket.

'We're listening.' Jack coaxed.

'Releasing the information will do two things. It will tell them Heather isn't worth targeting anymore because we have other evidence. We don't know if they know what's on the recording, but we know they believe it will incriminate them.'

'Following so far.' Jack encouraged her to continue.

'They have two choices now. Run or eliminate us all. I know which one I'd choose.'

'Bridges, get on to that background check now. Make sure none of our suspects try to leave the country. I'll warn Anderson. The AFP need to know we might have a runner heading to Botswana.'

'How do we stop them trying to knock us all off instead?' Max tapped his foot as he waited to get Heather out of the building and keep her safe.

'I don't think they'll be that stupid, but everyone should keep their eyes wide open. Everyone.' Jack looked at all the faces staring back at him. 'Liz, I'll go with you to the jewellers.' Max chuckled and left with Heather.

'If we drive them underground, how on earth are we going to catch the killer?' Bridges rolled his chair back to his desk and coaxed his computer screen to life.

'We'll have to tackle this on a few fronts Bridges. Let's hope something pops soon. I'm not ruling out some undercover work. What do you think Williams?'

'I'd say bring it on.'

23

Jenny's phone buzzed in her pocket. She answered it and Jack turned to Liz, who had sat back down on the corner of his desk. He dropped his marker pen on the desktop and leant in so only she could hear him.

'Are you available for dinner tonight?'

'Come over to my place. I'll cook something. I don't feel like going out.' She winked, stood up and collected the folder and her backpack from his desk.

'Do you want to leave that here?' He indicated the folder. She shook her head.

'No. I'd like to mull over it a bit on the weekend. Do a little digging into the jewellers and maybe the De Beers and Van der Standt by the sound of it.'

'I was thinking you might be ready for that surfing lesson I promised you?'

'I don't know Jack. The weather is still pretty chilly.'

'I've got a wetsuit that would fit you.'

Jenny hung up and broke into their conversation. 'That was Anderson.'

Liz welcomed the distraction. She didn't want to say no to Jack, but it really was too cold to be getting wet just yet and besides, for the first time in a long time she felt like learning something new might be a little overwhelming.

'What has he got?' Jack took his eyes from hers and fixed them on Jenny.

'He said he's found us an investigator in Botswana that can try and find Taiwo, but he also dug up something interesting about the De Beer Game Reserve.' She looked from Liz to Jack.

'Don't keep me hanging Williams.'

'Sorry Boss. The game reserve was under federal investigation years ago, back before...'

'Before Marilyn's death.'

Jenny nodded. 'It turns out the investigation went cold after her death, so nothing came of it.'

'What were they investigating them for?' Liz was even more determined to dig online when she got home now.

'Anderson doesn't know yet. He's going to see if he can pull the file and if the Botswana police officer looking for Taiwo can shed any light on it.'

'Good work.' Jack stood up to show Liz out. 'See if any of the jewellers we have on our list are looking for staff.' He placed his hand on the small of Liz's back. 'I'll show you out.'

'I know the way Detective.' She grinned. 'I'll also see if I can get a reference for Jenny from Robert. It might help get her into one of the jewellery stores.'

She saw Jack hesitate. 'Is that a good idea? Robert Glover might not be squeaky clean.'

'True, but you don't honestly expect to be lucky enough to find one of the jewellers hiring?'

Jack shrugged. 'Cleaning staff maybe?' She rolled her eyes at him. 'Okay, you win. Watch him closely thought Liz, he could be involved.'

'I'll be careful.' She touched his serious lips as he pressed the elevator call button. 'I'll quiz him about your less than cooperative HR guy too. What was his name?'

'Gregory. When did you want to go ring shopping?' The elevator doors opened.

'Tomorrow mid-morning would be good. They should all be open on a Saturday morning. We can grab breakfast and go after that.' She wasn't assuming Jack would stay the night, but she hoped he would.

'See you when I finish here.' She thought he might kiss her, but the elevator doors threatened to close and he put his hand over them to keep them open.

'See you then.'

24

Jack barely got a foot in the office before Bridges bailed him up. 'Got that list of company directors and managers for all the jewellers.' He handed Jack a piece of paper.

'Good work.' Bridges seemed to appreciate the compliment and Jack couldn't help but wonder why the guy suddenly wanted his approval. When he'd first arrived, he'd been aloof, disinterested in getting involved in anything that might turn out to be a career make or break case.

He made a mental note to ask the Chief about Bridges' real story and why he'd been forced to take a job in Adelaide instead of Sydney. When the guy first arrived, Jack had thought he was Internal Affairs. They'd just had two dirty cops unearthed, and one was shot by Williams. But it became quickly obvious the guy was just a replacement detective and one who didn't give much away in conversation.

'He's eager.' Jenny whispered as Jack sat down opposite her.

Jack shrugged. 'Makes for a nice change.' She grinned.

'Anything interesting?' She peered over toward the list. Jack looked at it, taking in the names one at a time.

'Nothing stands out, but we can ask Anderson to cross reference them with Immigration and Customs.'

'Have we got enough to open this investigation up to the AFP to take over?'

'I'd rather not, unless we are forced to. This is personal Williams.'

Jenny nodded. 'I get it. But Anderson could really do a lot more to help if this was officially his case.'

'Did you find any *Wanted* ads with any of the jewellers?' Jack changed the subject and watched as Jenny took the hint.

'Nothing yet. I'll keep an eye out. Maybe you can tell me which one to focus on after you go ring shopping.' She grinned and Jack rolled his eyes.

'I think you'll need to shop for a ring before me Williams.'

'I don't know.' The singing tone she used made Jack shiver.

'You have such a vivid imagination.' Jack's phone rang and he couldn't help but be relieved at the interruption. Jenny grinned knowingly. How could he expect anything else? He was surrounded by investigators. It was only a matter of time before he and Liz were going to have to come clean.

'Check and see if the site manager has that info we need and see if George Baxter is in, don't tell them why,' he added as he looked at the caller ID. 'Anderson. Thanks for calling back mate.'

'No worries bro. Sorry I called Williams before. Killing two birds with one stone, you know.' Jack didn't say anything, but he knew what it was like to be involved with someone who you worked closely with.

'Anyway. I've done some more digging since I spoke with Williams. Pretty interesting stuff. My guy in Botswana hasn't found Taiwo Moremi yet, but he's managed to find her brother.' He let the silence linger and Jack resisted the urge to ask him to get on with it.

'I'm still digging into why the De Beer's place was under investigation, but Taiwo's brother, Kabo Moremi works for them.'

'That *is* interesting. Can your contact interview him?'

'Sorry bro. He's gone bush.'

'That's too big a coincidence.' Jenny looked up and Jack could see he'd piqued her interest. 'Can you track where the De Beers stayed each time they visited Adelaide and if they've been over here since?'

'I gave you all the dates they've ever visited in that list. They haven't been back to Australia since she died.'

'Okay, time I gave them a call.' He looked at his watch doing a quick time calculation in his head. 'Can you track down where they stayed? Just see if anything pops out as strange. Appointments, referees they gave on their immigration statements?'

'I'll see what I can do Jack, but my boss is starting to ask questions. Marilyn was still a South African citizen when she was murdered. I'll be under pressure to hand this over to their authorities soon if you can't nail it down.'

'Why?'

'Someone's asking questions from the top down.'

'Are they? That's interesting. Any ideas who?'

'Nah bro. I'll see if I can uncover anything though.'

'Thanks. You guys doing anything for dinner Sunday night?'

'I don't think so. Ask Jenny.'

'Will do mate. See ya soon.' Jack hung up and looked at Jenny who'd been eavesdropping on the conversation.

'Are you and Hemi free for dinner Sunday? My place?'

'Sure. Business or personal?'

'A bit of both.'

'Sounds good. You inviting Max and the midget?'

'You mean Liz or Heather?'

'Oh, don't let her hear you say that. She'll flatten you.'

'I have no doubt. They'll all be there. At least they'll all get an invite.' Jack did a quick search on the internet to find out the time zone difference between Adelaide and Botswana. 'Let's hope we don't get any more call outs this weekend.'

'Fingers crossed.'

Jenny returned her attention to her computer screen as Jack searched the internet for the De Beer's Game Reserve contact information and scrolled through pages as he dialled the number on his desk phone. The dial tone changed pitch as it went through the police switchboard. Jack continued looking at photos as the phone rang.

The *About* page showed a family photo of the De Beers with a son and daughter, neither of whom were Marilyn. He'd had no idea Marilyn had siblings and the thought made him realise he must have been way too absorbed in his own work when he lived with her.

'Oasis Reserve.' The accent made memories flood back into Jack's mind. The woman even sounded like Marilyn. 'Tash speaking.'

'Hi Tash. Just wondering if I can speak with Mr or Mrs De Beer?'

'I'm sorry, but neither of them are here at present. Can I help you? I'm Tash De Beer.'

Jack was thrown, but only for a heartbeat. Sister? Sister-in-law? 'Thanks Tash. I'm not sure if you know me or not. This might seem very strange.' He wasn't sure if it would feel the same for Tash but it certainly was surreal to him. It had been ten years since Marilyn went missing and not one person, Tash included had spoken to him about her disappearance.

The woman waited patiently. 'My name is Jack Cunningham.' He listened for any sign she knew who he was. Nothing. 'I'm a detective in Adelaide, Australia.' His accent was likely a dead giveaway, but it was surprising how many people got the southern states accent mixed up with English or New Zealanders.

'What can I do for you Detective?' Not a hint of who he was, or what Adelaide meant to her family.

'Are you a De Beer by marriage Tash?' It seemed the logical answer.

Jenny stopped typing, her eyes scanned his face for a clue as to what was going on at the other end of the phone. Jack didn't notice, he was so thrown by hearing Marilyn had a sister or sister-in-law.

'No Detective.' She sounded annoyed. 'I've kept my maiden name.' Not unheard of but she seemed a little arrogant over it.

'I've got some bad news. I thought the authorities might have already contacted your parents, but since I haven't heard from anyone, I'm guessing maybe they haven't.' Silence. She wasn't giving anything away, or maybe she didn't know anything.

'Your sister, Marilyn's remains have been found recently.' Not a gasp, not a sound. Maybe she was in shock? 'She's been murdered Ms De Beer.' It sounded strange to use the title Marilyn was often referred to by.

'Thank you for letting me know Detective. I'll be sure to pass the information on to my parents.' That's it, not a tear, not a word of outrage at not being informed. He wanted to jump on a plane then and there and find out what the hell had happened between Marilyn and her family for her sister to not give a shit about discovering she had been murdered.

'If your parents would like any information, please give them my number. I'll be available to discuss the ongoing homicide investigation with them.'

'I'll be sure to tell them Detective.' The line went dead. Jack stared at the receiver and slowly replaced it.

'That was just plain weird.'

'Sounded weird.' Jenny tapped a file on the desk to realign the contents before adding it to a stack next to her desk phone.

'That was Marilyn's sister Tash.' He knew his tone sounded ludicrous, but Jenny said nothing. 'I didn't know she had a sister.'

'Seems there is a lot you didn't know about Marilyn De Beer Jack. When exactly did she immigrate?'

'I thought it was a few years before we met, but Liz showed me the letters, dated over twenty years ago. The handwriting on the letters from her friend Taiwo looked young. Do we have an age on Taiwo?'

Jenny grabbed her mouse and tapped it to bring her screen back to life.

'DOB is 28th July nineteen-seventy-five.'

'So twenty nineteen now makes her forty-four. Same age as Marilyn. School friends maybe?'

'You should have asked Tash.' The sarcasm was rife as Jenny stood to open her desk drawer and retrieve her handbag. She checked her gun safety was on and locked it back in the drawer. She seldom took it home for the weekend, not unless they were expecting any issues.

'Very funny. I might chat with Liz about doing some digging into the De Beer family history this weekend. We'll see what Google has to say about them.'

Jack got up to leave, grabbed his jacket from the back of his chair and retrieved his weapon from his locked drawer, placing it into his holster after checking the safety.

'You expecting trouble?' Jenny made her way to the hallway and the elevator.

'I've just got a feeling about this case Williams. I'm not sure why, but we organised that press release for tonight's news.' He looked at his watch. 'Our abductor and possible clean up man could be on the prowl for answers to what we know.'

'Good point.' Jenny nodded and returned to her desk, unlocked the drawer and retrieved her own weapon. She placed it back into her shoulder holster and strapped it back in place before tossing her handbag over the other shoulder. 'There were three people involved in Heather's attempted abduction. The driver, plus the two in the back. No one turned up seeking medical help, so we've got no idea who they are.'

'True. Even more reason to take your weapon home for the weekend. Three henchmen, all happy to kidnap a young woman. Got to wonder how the De Beer family have managed to organise that much muscle here.'

'Maybe it isn't them? Maybe it's whoever their Australian contacts are that are covering everything up.' Jenny moved toward the hallway.

'Monday, we interview Baxter and anyone who might have knowledge of that building site demolition order.'

Jenny nodded. 'You coming?'

'In a sec.' Jack stopped by Bridges' desk and Jenny continued into the hallway. 'Might pay to take your gun home this weekend Bridges. The detective looked up, a frown crossing his rounded face, making his receding hairline even more prominent.

'If you say so.' The tone was what Jack had come to expect from Bridges, but the detective retrieved his weapon just the same.

Jack suddenly realised the guy must be lonely since moving to Adelaide. Widowed, without kids according to Jenny, he kept to himself, but he was finally making an effort on this case. Maybe it was time Jack did the same.

'Mate. I'm having a get together at my place Sunday night if you're interested in catching up with the crew. A bit of a debrief, but mostly a social catch up.' Bridges clipped his holster strap over his weapon and looked over at Jack, his expression unreadable. For a second Jack thought he'd tell him to rack off, but his features relaxed into a rare smile.

'Thanks.' He tidied his desk up as he spoke. 'I'd like that.'

'See you then. I'll text you the details.' Jack left with a wave, thinking about how things had changed in such a short time. Just over six months before he'd been working with Max, putting up with the cranky, caffeine addicted smart-arse first thing in the morning and arguing over him throwing his cigarette butts out the window, to working with Jenny as his partner and a whole new team of detectives now that Rickard was in prison and Johnnie was dead.

Now, as he took the stairs to the parking garage he thought about Liz. If someone had told him he'd be dating a former escort come PI who still ran an escort agency, he would have thought they'd lost their mind, but that was exactly what he was doing. And for the first time in a long time he couldn't be more sure of anything.

He knew he was a little OCD and liked his ducks all in a row, but Liz had opened him up to the spontaneous. She was even reckless at times and he was beginning to embrace the feeling. Now it was his turn to return the favour. He chuckled as he considered how Liz was going to go learning to surf on Sunday. Now all he needed to do was convince her that if he could embrace a new lifestyle, so could she.

25

Liz opened her oven, stepping back a moment to allow the wave of basil and tomato laced steam to dissipate before pulling the rack out and poking a skewer into the lasagne. The skewer gave way through the béchamel sauce and layered toppings. Satisfied it was ready, she closed the oven and turned it off.

Reaching for her laptop, she opened her *Foxy Escort Agencies* email account, searching recent emails for the one she was looking for. It was marked *unread*, which should have made it easy to find, but she'd been a little side-tracked lately and the unread list was piling up.

She wondered how much longer she could juggle so many balls, but part of her knew Foxy would be hanging around for a while longer in one shape or form. Jack would just have to deal with the fact he was dating a Madam.

Liz clicked the mousepad and opened the email from Stephanie Miles. It hadn't surprised Liz to find it in her inbox only a day after visiting the *Guild and Glover* office and meeting the tall, gorgeous receptionist.

She read quickly, finding the phone number she was hoping for at the bottom of the email. Retrieving her mobile, she dialled and waited. As the phone rang, she reached above her stove and got out two long stem red wine glasses.

'Stephanie. It's Lillian Fox. Do you have a second to talk?' Liz could hear loud music in the background, along with the hum of loud voices and guessed Stephanie was out for drinks on a Friday night like most single females should be.

'Sure, give me a sec to get out of this noise.' She spoke loudly, for her own benefit more than Liz's. The background hustle slowly gave way to the hollow sound that one usually related to a bathroom. 'What can I do for you?' The woman's voice rattled around the tiled room.

'Well, I've got two hats on for this call Stephanie. I hope you don't mind. Number one, I got your email and I'm so pleased you contacted me. My business partner Connie will be in contact with you soon to go over how we get you started. We have a few hours of training that we need to go through.'

'What kind of training?' Liz smiled at the tone. All the girls and even a few of the guys she employed had reacted similarly.

'It's not sex training so don't panic. We all have our own style of seduction.' Liz laughed to ease the tension. 'We offer a few hours of do's and don'ts for safety protocol and we also have mandatory health check-ups that are required. Connie will just go over all the tedious details with you. But, if you do have questions about the trade, please don't be shy in asking them. Connie has been in the game nearly as long as me and she will be only too happy to share her stories.'

'Oh. Thanks. What was the second hat?'

'Your company are doing my books now, so you'll likely know soon enough but I'm also a private investigator and I have a little favour I'd like to ask you.' Liz waited, no reply and she suddenly realised her request might feel a little like coercion. 'You don't have to do this to be part of the team, not at all. I want to make that perfectly clear. This is more a case of looking out for the fairer sex. Do you know what I'm investigating?'

There was a moment of silence, a slow breath, the sound of dripping water in the background. 'I don't. Am I supposed to?'

'Not at all. Robert has obviously been very discrete. A girl that worked for *Guild and Glover* about ten years ago, went missing. She's been confirmed dead, murdered.' Liz waited and let the idea settle in. 'Us ladies need to stick together and I wanted to find out if anyone knew the woman back then—someone who would be willing to share any insights. In particular, if the woman's family ever visited her at work.'

'I have to admit, all this is a little overwhelming Liz, ah Lillian.'

'Call me Liz, if it makes life easier. I'm not working for the agency anymore. I just run it.'

'Oh. Any reason?' Liz felt herself blush, just before the door buzzer sounded. She looked at her watch.

'Well, it's a long story. I'll tell you over coffee one day.' She moved to the security tablet on her counter and checked the person at the door was Jack. She was greeted by him waving another bottle of wine in front of the lens.

'Look, I need to go. I'll email you the information and you tell me if you want to help or not. Like I said,' she moved to the door and opened it, 'this isn't mandatory. You decide and either way, it won't have any impact on our other arrangement. Okay?'

Jack looked at her strangely, but said nothing as she moved away from the open door and back to her computer. Jack closed the door behind him.

'Okay. It sounds fine. Send me the details and I'll decide once I see what you need.'

'Of course. Thanks Stephanie. Talk soon.'

'Bye.' Liz hung up and placed her mobile on the counter.

'Another bottle of wine.' Liz moved forward, taking it from Jack's hand and placing it on the counter safely, before wrapping her arms around his neck and smothering his lips with hers. At first, she thought he was going to ask questions over her kisses, but his body relaxed with each passing second.

Picking her up, he nearly knocked the bottle from the counter as he placed her firmly on top. She giggled and he pulled back a moment, his eyes scanning hers.

'I like it when you smile.'

'I like it when I smile too.' He moved forward, touching his lips to her neck, sending tingles down to her toes.

'Something smells delicious.'

'Lasagne,' she answered as he reached his hand under her tight-fitting sport top.

'That wasn't what I could smell.' His hand reached her breast and she gasped as he pinched the nipple gently.

'Dinner is ready,' she whispered.

'That's exactly what I was thinking.' His voice was raspy as his hand moved down between her legs and his fingers found their way inside her yoga shorts.

****

'You know your lasagne is likely cold now.' Liz grinned as she rolled on top of him and he pulled her to his chest, the smell of sweat and aftershave going straight to her nether regions.

'I didn't think you could eat pasta,' he smiled as she brushed his lips with hers.

'Gluten free.' She bit his lip gently. 'As much as I want to devour you again, I am starving.'

'Have to admit. I missed lunch again and the smell of basil is growing a little more alluring now.'

'Now that your basic appetites are sated.'

'Oh, we barely touched the surface, but a guy has to refuel you know.'

'I know.' Liz jumped out of bed and swayed her hips purposefully as she made her way to the bathroom. 'But I need a shower first.' She wrapped her naked leg around the door frame, squeezing her breast against the wood and pouted. 'You coming in?'

Jack threw back his head and laughed. 'Am I coming in? What kind of question is that?' He was out of bed and dragging her into the bathroom so fast, she nearly slipped over.

'You know you might never have used your womanly charms on me before, but you are certainly making up for it now.'

Liz stepped into the large walk-in shower and turned the water on. Sitting down on the steam bench, she beckoned him to her. His energy recovery was obvious. As he knelt between her legs she whispered. 'I'm all yours, Detective.' He grinned up at her before he whispered back.

'Lucky I'm still hungry.'

****

'Cold lasagne is fine.'

'Nope, never.' Liz cut a few portions and placed them in her steam oven, setting the temperature before pressing the timer. 'I had this all planned and you totally ruined it.' She waved her arms theatrically before reaching for a bottle of red wine she'd opened just before he arrived. 'At least this has had plenty of time to breathe.'

He chuckled. 'At least one of us has.'

'Oh, stop complaining.' She moved around the counter, two glasses in hand. 'We have work to do.'

'What work?' He took the wine and sipped it.

'We need to go over our cover story for engagement ring shopping tomorrow.'

'Not too hard.' He took another sip of red wine. 'This is good.'

'I know.' Liz took a sip. 'Okay Detective, what's our cover?'

'Nothing to it. First names only, looking for ethical diamonds. How do we know they are legit? You talk, I'll scope out the staff.'

'Why don't you talk and I'll scope?'

'Because everyone always pays attention to the pretty woman in the room.' The oven timer buzzed and Liz moved to get their dinner out.

'Flattery will get you everywhere.'

'I made a weird call today.'

'To who?' Liz put the warmed lasagne onto two plates that were already loaded with salad.

'I rang Marilyn's parents. Got her sister.'

'Did you know she had a sister?' Cutlery was added to the plates before Liz moved them both to the other side of the sparkling white stone kitchen counter.

'Nope. I've never spoken to her parents before. Marilyn never said anything about them and I never pushed.'

'Want to do some internet stalking?' Liz grinned mischievously as she cut the first piece of pasta and placed it in her mouth.

'If you don't mind?'

'Since when have I not liked sticking my nose into other people's business?' Liz looked genuinely shocked he'd asked the question.

'Good point.' He saluted with his wine glass.

'You're not supposed to agree you know.'

'Oh sorry. You don't exactly come with instructions.'

Ten minutes later Jack was doing dishes while Liz tapped keys on her laptop. 'Okay, the De Beers have owned the Oasis Game Reserve for over fifty years, but it wasn't always a game reserve. Here, look at this.'

Liz spun the laptop around and Jack whistled. A photo of a group of what looked like western tourists, all dressed in army camo greeted them. At their feet lay a large lion, its throat cut, blood pooling below the neck and soaking into the sand.

'When was that taken?' Jack wiped the final plate and put it away, hanging the tea-towel neatly on the oven door rail before joining Liz.

'I'm not sure.' She clicked a few more buttons. 'Does this guy look familiar?' Liz pointed to a man in his early twenties, with blonde hair and a cheesy smile.

'I don't know. We probably need to blow the picture up or get a better version of it. Who took it?'

'It's a promotional photo, taken about twenty years ago. It's not currently on their website, but someone tagged the resort, before it was a reserve so it came up in the search.'

'Well big game trophy hunting was legal back then in Botswana. What site is the photo on?' Jack reached for the bottle of wine and topped up Liz's glass before adding the rest to his own.

'It's legal again in Botswana.' Liz opened an article on her laptop and Jack began to read.

'No way. I didn't realise.'

'This year, the new President lifted the ban. Said that the wildlife was interacting with human populations too often, causing damage to cropping land, the death of livestock and almost as often, the mauling or death of humans.'

'So, have the De Beers returned to Trophy Hunting?'

'I think the better question might be, did they ever stop?'

26

Liz stood outside the window of *Elegant and Elite* and stared at the array of pink, yellow and white diamonds. Jack placed his hand on the small of her back and guided her through the doorway.

Elegant and Elite weren't the average jewellery store, with long glass cabinets and sales staff in black and white attire. They were wholesale jewellers, who offered a small display of custom pieces either side of a counter that looked like it came from an old Western movie, complete with dark wooden fluted corbels and jailhouse bars like an old-style bank teller window.

Two jewellers in their late sixties worked on separate tables behind the counter. Large magnifying lights hovered over gold and diamond studded rings held in tiny vice-like devices with soldering irons and clamps scattered around the tables.

The counter had two windows, occupied by two equally plain looking women. One had her almost black hair tied back in a loose ponytail. The other wore her greying brunette locks loose. Neither bothered with makeup or fine clothing. Instead opting for cotton shirts and plain black dress pants.

'Can I help you?' the greying woman asked as Jack and Liz entered the small room, with aged green carpet and no windows. The studio was on the third floor of an otherwise unremarkable building on a side alley from the hustle and bustle of Rundle Mall. If you hadn't known it was there, you'd never have stumbled upon it by accident.

'Yes, thanks. I'm Liz, this is my fiancé Jack.'

'Pleased to meet you.' The woman waited patiently, a friendly smile on her lips.

'I'd like to get a quote on a custom engagement ring but I don't really know where to start. I have a few photos of rings I like.' Liz pulled out the magazine articles she'd found with Marilyn's possessions.

'Oh, these are quite dated. Are you sure you'd like something like this?'

'Jewellery dates?' Jack spoke for the first time. The woman's smile deepened.

'It does Sir. Like any fashion item, trends come and go.'

'Oh.'

'I see one of these is ours.' The woman pointed to the advert from *Elegant and Elite*. 'Terry made this one.' She picked up the article and turned around to the jeweller on the left. 'Didn't you Terry?' There was something in her tone that made Jack's posture stiffen slightly and both he and Liz studied the jeweller more closely.

'I've made thousands of rings Patricia.' He waved her back to her work, but not before he'd taken an earnest look at the piece of paper.

'How do we know the diamonds used in your rings are ethical diamonds?' Liz offered the question lightly, but there was something in Terry's eyes that she didn't miss. That and the few heartbeats it took for Patricia to answer the question were all the confirmation she and Jack needed that they were in the right place.

'Oh, only ethical diamonds are imported into Australia these days. It's legislation.'

'So, all your diamonds come with authenticity papers and a chain of custody log through the ethical diamond agreement?'

'Oh, you are well versed.' A nervous giggle. 'That's exactly right. Or you can opt for a lab grown diamond if it makes you feel more comfortable.'

'Why would I be more comfortable with a fake diamond, if you can assure me the real ones are ethical?'

'No reason,' Patricia answered quickly. 'None at all, of course.' She tried to smooth it over.

'Look. I really like this pink diamond, but if the style is dated, and you don't want to make an older style ring, I think I might have to think about it.' Liz put the pieces of paper back in her Prada backpack and tossed it over one shoulder. 'Honey. Let's go grab a late breakie.' Liz took Jack's hand and turned to leave.

She fully expected the woman to stop her, like most sales people would—offer to make her whatever she wanted. But Patricia and Terry couldn't wait to see the back of her which only further fuelled the sinking feeling she had in her stomach.

They took the narrow staircase down to the ground floor and stepped out through the painted glass door to the alleyway.

'Well that was pretty interesting.'

'Certainly was. Did you see Terry's face when Patricia showed him that ring?'

'He went pale.'

'And when I asked about ethical diamonds straight afterward, I thought Patricia might faint.'

'Is this what Marilyn had found out? Would it really be enough to get her killed?'

'More importantly, are her parents tied up in an *un*ethical diamond smuggling ring and if they are, would they be willing to kill their daughter over it?'

27

'I'm bored out of my head here. Your internet speed sucks big time.' Heather stood up from the old worn recliner and picked up her bag. 'And I've slept on this shitty chair too many nights now. I'm going home.'

Max jumped up, the milk from his cereal sloshing into his lap as he got to his feet. He put the bowl down on the kitchen bench as he pursued Heather, swiping at the milk stain as he moved. 'We only just released the information about your recording yesterday. You can't go home yet.'

'Of course I can. You can stay at my place if you insist on playing bodyguard. Besides, I need to do some washing, refresh my make-up, deodorant, underwear, tampons.'

'La la la. I don't need to know that stuff.'

'I thought you had a daughter?'

'I do, but I only met her six months ago. She was adopted out when we were young.' Heather's face paled, if that was even possible with all the light coloured Gothic foundation she wore. 'I didn't know! Liz never told me!' He knew he sounded defensive.

'I don't care!' Heather stuffed her phone in her bag and moved to the door. 'Either you come with me or I'll call an Uber.'

'Okay, okay. You win. Let me grab a few things and text Jack what we are doing.'

'Why? I don't answer to him.'

'No, but I do.' Max left the small living area and grabbed an overnight bag, stuffing it with the essentials that were scattered around his untidy bedroom. He reasoned he could always come back and pick up a few extra items on the way to Jack's Sunday tonight.

When he reached the living area again, Heather was already gone. Mumbling under his breath, he grabbed his car keys, wallet and locked the flat door. He nearly twisted his ankle as he tripped over the lifted crack in the concrete. A timely reminder that he needed to find a new place to live.

When he reached his car in the rear car parking area and stopped, a cold shiver ran down his spine, shooting out via his feet like a lightning strike. Heather wasn't standing impatiently outside his car, tapping her foot like she usually did. Heather was nowhere in sight.

'Heather! Where the fuck *are* you?' He looked behind the row of bins, around past his silver Mazda and his neighbour's old Renault. 'Come on you little pain in the arse. I'm not paid enough to deal with your shit.'

No answer. The cold shiver turned into a solid rock in his gut as he fished frantically for his mobile phone. He pressed the button on his keys and moved around to open the driver's side door, the wait as he listened to the ringing was torturous, but when Jack answered the phone, Max suddenly wished a hole would open and swallow him up.

'What's up? You good for tomorrow night?'

'Heather is gone!'

'Gone like for a walk or gone like kidnapped gone?' Jack's tone wasn't panicked yet, but it would be any second, Max knew it.

'We were just about to head to her place. She needed stuff. I went and grabbed something out of my room and when I came back out, she was gone. I figured she was just being her usual impatient self, waiting by the car, you know, toe tapping, hands on hips, like Liz does.' He was rambling.

'Slow down mate. We'll find her.'

'I fucked up Jack.'

'What was she doing when she told you she needed stuff from home?'

Max sat down behind the wheel of his car as his phone pinged with a text.

'Hang on.' He slid Jack's call to the side of his phone so he could talk and read the text at the same time. 'Little bitch.'

'What?' Jack's voice sounded as Max flicked the text screen sideways and opened his call screen once more.

'She's gone to meet someone. Said don't worry, she'll be fine.'

'We need to trace that last text Max. Get to Liz's. I'll call in a favour from Anderson.'

'Will do mate. I'll try calling her back. I'm sorry I lost her.'

'Don't be mate. She's a mini Liz and we both know how much trouble that can cause.' Max heard Liz protest next to him, complete with a slap on his arm he would bet his life on it, but it wasn't putting a smile on his face. Why the hell would she go off alone like that?

'I'll get there as soon as I can. I'll spin by her house just in case.'

'Don't run any red lights. Anderson will take a while to get us that phone record.'

Max was just about to hang up. 'Shit!'

'What?'

'Heather's phone is still in my car. How the hell did she just text me?' Then it dawned on him. 'She must have had a second phone.'

'It's okay. We'll ping a few cell towers and see who made calls around that time.'

'Getting a warrant for that will be impossible.'

'It's okay. Liz knows a guy, remember.'

'Scott! Shit I hope he can find her. I've got a really bad feeling about this mate.'

'You and me both Max.'

28

Jack dialled Anderson's number as soon as Max hung up.

'What's going on?' Liz watched Jack's face contort with what looked like genuine pain.

'I'll explain in a second.' The phone continued to ring. 'Pick up mate.'

'I'll try Jenny.' Liz retrieved her phone from her backpack and clicked on her recent calls. Jenny's number was only three from the top. She pressed redial.

'It's Jack mate, give me a call. It's urgent.'

'Now tell me what's going on.'

'Heather did a runner.'

'Stupid girl.'

'Hey, hang on there.' Jenny answered her phone.

'Not you. Is Anderson with you?'

'Ah.'

'It's urgent.' Liz rushed over the hesitation in Jenny's voice. 'I'll pass Jack over.'

'Anderson?'

'I'm just getting him. Don't you people have a life?'

'Heather has taken off. I need Anderson to check on a few things for me.'

'I'm here. What do you need?'

'Heather ducked out on Max. She's left her phone in Max's car, which means she's likely picked up a burner. I know you can't help with that. But can you check her normal phone? She might have received a text message on it before getting a pre-paid?'

'I'll see what I can do. Where are we meeting?'

'Liz's place. We need to pool our resources to find this kid, before she gets herself killed.'

'On it mate. We'll be there in ten.'

Jack hung up. 'Let's get back to your place. I can't believe she split like that. Who the hell is she meeting and where?'

'I'll see if I can wake Scott. He's not usually up for hours yet.'

'Damn. I forgot he was a night owl.'

'Vampire more like it.' Liz dialled his number. 'Scott. Call me when you get this message. It's life and death or I wouldn't bother you.' She hung up, sent out a few text messages and put her phone back in her pocket, not bothering with her bag as they both walked at maximum pace back through the roadway along Charles Street past David Jones department store towards North Terrace and Liz's apartment.

There were some advantages to living in the city and a short distance between shops and entertainment were just a few, but Liz was particularly glad about it today.

'Who did you text?'

'A few of his acquaintances that I know. Maybe one of them can coax him out of bed early.'

Liz's phone rang and she retrieved it as they left Charles Street and turned down North Terrace. 'Scott. Thanks for getting back to me. Sorry about the early call.'

'It's okay. What's up?'

'Max has been watching a girl who was a victim of an attempted kidnapping. All good until she just gave Max the slip.'

'Why would she do that?'

'Long story, but the short version is she's been investigating a case which we are also working on and it looks like she's organised to meet with someone, without telling any of us. We need to track her down.'

'What's her name.'

'Heather Johnston.'

'Heather. No way.'

'You know her?'

'Yeah. I know her. She leaves a digital footprint like a friggin' elephant. I'll find her.' Scott's tone didn't give away much. Was it frustration or admiration she could hear in his voice?

'Thanks Scott. It's pretty time sensitive. Do you need her mobile number?'

'Send it through, but I should be able to track her down pretty quickly.' It sounded like Scott was more than familiar with Heather's movements.

'Thanks.' Liz hung up as they entered Liz's apartment building foyer. 'Hi Bennie.'

'Good morning Ms Jeffreys.' The doorman come security guard waved to Jack as they passed by, giving him a wink that offered approval that they were obviously seeing each other regularly. 'Nice day out there isn't it?'

'Could be better Bennie, but yes, the weather is good.' Liz moved past, scanned her card at the elevator and waited for the doors to open.

'Scott seemed to know Heather. I guess the Goth should have given it away. Maybe they move in the same circles.' Liz stepped into the elevator, Jack followed close behind.

'Oh Bennie,' Liz stuck her head back out the elevator door, peering around the wall as the doorman turned to the sound of her voice, 'I have a tribe of visitors coming. Can you please scan them all into the elevator?'

'Sure thing.' Bennie waved as Liz let the elevator doors close.

'How would you feel if I included Bridges in this briefing?'

Liz shrugged. 'I think the line in the sand went out the window when Jenny and Hemi started coming around.'

'It's just that he's part of the case now and I should at least give him the option to join in chasing down Heather.'

'You don't need to explain. I get it. Besides, I don't think your place is big enough for that many people. There's only so many large bodies we can squeeze around that little oak table of yours.' Liz smiled as the elevator doors opened on her floor.

'I'll call him now.'

29

Liz felt like pouring a large glass of wine, her nerves were so rattled, but it wasn't even lunchtime yet. 'I can't believe she could be so stupid.'

'Reminds me of someone I know.' Jack's tone was flat, but the corner of his eye twinkled with mild amusement.

'Oh shut up. I'm nearly fifty, she's barely out of her teens.'

'I'm not sure age has anything to do with it. She's just headstrong.'

Liz huffed, not sure if she was frustrated by Jack's comments or Heather's disappearance more. 'I hope she's okay. Scott thinks he can track her digital footprint fairly easily, not sure how quickly though.'

'She told Max she was meeting someone. We can only assume it has something to do with the case, so who could she be meeting with, that we haven't already questioned?'

'Good point. Hold that thought until everyone else gets here and maybe we can sort this mess out. Is Bridges coming?'

'Yep, he replied to the text I sent him with your address.'

'Good. It's about time we got to the bottom of why he is even in Adelaide. I'll coax it out of him.'

Jack chuckled, the idea of Liz interrogating Bridges obviously amusing him. The buzzer sounded and Jack moved toward the door. Liz didn't bother looking at the security camera. She knew Jack was still armed and it was likely Jenny and Hemi anyway.

'Kia Ora brothers and sisters.'

'There's only two of them Hemi.' Jenny admonished the big Kiwi who only shrugged, showing little concern.

The change in his personality since joining the team and dating Jenny had been nothing short of miraculous. Liz smiled as she recalled Jenny ranting about the Australian Federal Police officer with nothing but contempt after their first few meetings. They'd locked horns over case jurisdiction but once they all got to know Hemi, they realised he was just passionate about his work like all of them were.

'I come bearing gifts.' Hemi grinned, the white of his teeth more obvious against his darkened skin and traditional tattoos.

'I could do with something positive. What have you got?' Liz asked as she moved to turn the coffee machine on. 'Coffee everyone?'

A chorus of 'yes' greeted the sound of the door buzzer. Jack stood to open the door.

'I should probably wait for everyone to arrive hey?' Hemi looked across the kitchen counter as Bridges entered.

Jenny looked from Bridges to Liz, eyebrow raised. Liz nodded slightly before turning to greet the new arrival.

'Bridges! Coffee?'

'If it isn't too much hassle?'

'Of course not. How do you have it?'

'No sugar, anything white is fine.'

'Latte it is then.'

'I'll help.' Jenny jumped up, rounded the counter from the opposite side to Bridges and moved up alongside Liz, grabbing coffee mugs from a cupboard to the left of the machine. 'Why is he here?' She snuck a peak over her shoulder.

'Because Jack has him on the investigation and he needs to know Heather has gone walk-about.'

'We could have briefed him Monday.'

'All hands, means all hands. Besides, I'm going to grill him about his Sydney days.' Jenny's creased brow was replaced by a wicked grin as she got a few more mugs out and placed them on the kitchen counter.

The coffee cycle finished and Liz picked up two lattes, taking one to Jack and the other over for Bridges. 'So, Bridges. You and I got off to a rocky start.' Liz was happy he had the good grace to blush since he'd called her all sorts of names when he had interviewed her over Ted's death.

'I'm sorry about that. It's part of the job.'

'Forget it. Past is the past. Although…'

The door buzzer sounded and Liz leant over and pressed the *unlock* button on her security system. It had to be Max and she was sick of people going back and forth to her door.

'Although, I would really like to hear more about Sydney before we finish up here today.' Bridges stopped sipping his coffee, the latte foam on his lip forgotten as he stared at Liz, unsure of exactly what to say in response. 'But what we have to share is a bit more important than cop shop gossip.'

Bridges relaxed as Max moved up next him to take the stool alongside. 'Don't fight it mate. She'll beat it out of you if she has to.' The solemn look on Max's face made Jenny laugh out loud, before everyone joined in. Bridges chuckled nervously, his eyes darting from Max to Liz still unsure.

'Okay, everyone is here. What you got Anderson?' Jack took charge and Liz listened as she put another two coffees on and opened the fridge to find some food.

'We know the De Beers have been to Australia before Marilyn died. Our contact in Botswana had advised that Taiwo is out of country and her visa information and passport say she is here, in Adelaide.'

'So that could be who Heather is meeting? I tried to call her back, but she's turned off her phone. That will make tracking her harder.' Max reached eagerly for the coffee Liz offered him, but she swerved at the last minute and put it down in front of

Jenny. Max pouted as the other coffee wafted under his nostrils on the way to Hemi.

'Or it could be who has been trying to shut her up? It is Taiwo's voice on that recording.' Jack got up to help Liz fix something for lunch, but she waved him back to his seat.

'Her address on the customs declaration was Heather's place at Saint Peters.' Hemi continued his report.

'That could be good or bad. Either way, the place is still empty, I drove past on the way here.' Max grinned like a kid as Liz placed a coffee on the countertop in front of him.

'Do we have mobile contact information for Taiwo?' Liz began making up a platter of dips and cheese to satisfy her impromptu guests. All she'd planned to do was spend the afternoon in bed with her favourite detective, so to say the fridge was bare was a bit of an understatement.

'She likely picked up a pre-paid sim when she arrived, but I can check.' Hemi pulled his mobile out of his pocket and moved away from the counter to find a quiet spot on the far side of Liz's living area.

Liz studied her pristine leather sofa, standing stately in front of the wide, modern fireplace. Less than a year ago, she'd thought her home was beautiful, like something seen in a Vogue magazine, but now she knew her apartment was sterile, devoid of life. Ironically Becca's death had brought warmth into her life. She looked around the room, listening to the chatter and smiled at the closeness she felt towards these people. A feeling she'd not known most of her life.

Jack touched her hand gently. 'You okay?' he whispered as he joined her in preparing food despite her earlier protest.

'I'm good.' She smiled, the sting of happy tears threatening to burst out. 'Let's focus on finding our runaway before she finds herself in harm's way.'

30

Hemi returned to the counter, plonking down on a stool beside Jenny, reaching for a piece of cheese and a thin wafer cracker.

'No go on the girl's phone. Our contact in Botswana is tracking down her brother but he did give me some interesting information on the De Beer investigation that got shelved all those years back.'

Jack felt a chill run down his back as he recalled Tash De Beer's disinterest in her sister's homicide investigation. He had yet to speak with Marilyn's parents.

'It seems the investigation was over a possible smuggling racket. The authorities in South Africa were deep into an investigation, apparently, they had a source, but no one seems to know who the source was. It wasn't in the investigation file.'

'Marilyn?' Jack sat back, the food on the counter forgotten as his stomach knotted and rolled. 'Maybe Marilyn was the source and that's what got her killed.'

'You're saying you think Marilyn's parents killed her? To avoid smuggling charges?' Liz touched his hand and Jack savoured the warmth.

'They visited just before she died.' His stomach knotted at the idea that keeping smuggling diamonds or game animals quiet would be enough to kill your own daughter.

'Do we know if any of the people on the list I compiled travelled to Botswana yet?' Bridges' tone was only mildly interested and Jack noticed he hadn't lost his appetite. Why would he? He had no interest in Marilyn's history.

'Anderson, if I get you all the names can you run them all through Immigration?' Jack knew he was asking a lot. This wasn't an official AFP investigation and he really hoped it wouldn't become one, but the closer they got to an international suspect, the more likely it was he'd have to hand the case over. At least he knew Hemi well enough to know he'd take care of the job personally.

'I'll see what I can find out.'

Jack watched Liz look at her smart watch and frown. Her phone buzzed silently on the far end of the long, kitchen counter.

She reached for the phone and Jack tried not to eavesdrop. 'Stephanie. I wasn't expecting a call on the weekend.'

It sounded like work, so he tried to tune out any details. Things were still very new and Liz might have given up her personal escort work, but he knew she hadn't dropped her role as Madam of *Foxy Escort Agencies*. What he didn't know was if it would cause them both ongoing hassles or not.

'Okay, that's really helpful Stephanie. Steph. Of course. Thanks. I'll be in touch. Soon. You're a gem.' She hung up, placed her phone on the counter and turned to see Jack studying her. He watched her face change from polite work mode to relaxed, then as she saw his face, a touch of frustration. Did she know what he was thinking? Probably.

The sound of discussion had turned to background murmuring as Jack had listened in on Liz's call. Now, as he focussed back on those around him, he heard the details of a discussion between Jenny and Bridges.

'Ivory exporting technically isn't illegal in South Africa.'

'Yes it is.' Jenny was arguing.

'No, it isn't.' Bridges hadn't raised his voice. He was just understatedly sure of himself. 'A number of African countries have shipped major stockpiles of Ivory to Japan. They say the funds are used for wildlife preservation.'

'That's horrific.'

'They've also reinstated Trophy Hunting licences.'

'Even worse.' Jenny was visibly appalled by the idea.

'It is to us, sure. But you try farming in a nation of starving people when elephants trample your crops and lions eat your workers.'

Jack could see the guy's point. How was culling lions any different from culling crocs in the far north?

'That would be fine if they actually used the produce to feed the poverty stricken in their own country, but they don't. They export the agricultural produce like any other nation—to the highest bidder.' Jack saw Hemi touch Jenny's leg as it jostled on the stool next to him.

'Hey. Australia and NZ do the same. It's the nature of Capitalism. Pretty easy to play armchair politics but when lions attack and kill your family, you might not be such an animal liberationist. Fortunately, our deadliest animal in NZ is a wild pig, unless you count spiders and magpies.' Hemi grinned. Jenny stared, like she'd been shocked into silence before shaking her head and chuckling under her breath, her shoulders relaxing, the leg jostling stopped.

'That was the receptionist from *Guild and Glover*.' Jack didn't want to know how Liz was on a first name basis with the woman. 'She quizzed Guild's private secretary. Apparently the woman was the receptionist back when Marilyn worked for the firm.'

'Anything helpful?' Jack reached for a handful of dried nuts and fruit, his appetite finally returning.

'Yes. More than I'd hoped or asked for. Marilyn only ever had one visitor to her work that the previous receptionist recalled and that was an African woman around her own age and, it gets better, *Guild and Glover* moved to the new fancy offices in North Adelaide, within a month of Marilyn's disappearance.'

'Even more reason to track down the movements of *Guild and Glover* staff.' Bridges wore a smug look and for the first time, Jack didn't feel like wiping it off his face.

31

'None of that helps us find Heather.' Max got up from the kitchen counter. 'If the African woman that visited Marilyn more ten years ago is Taiwo, then we need to know more about the woman that's been dropping clues in Heather's lap for the past few years.'

'I agree with Max. It could be a trap to tidy up loose ends, but Heather doesn't have anything but Taiwo's recording. Would that really be worth kidnapping her for?'

'No. There's something we are missing. We can link Marilyn to the three jewellers, and possibly blood diamonds, and the De Beers were under investigation for smuggling. So, are we assuming diamonds are still the key?' Liz picked up a white side plate and opened the dishwasher ready to put the dirty plate in.

'Possibly, but then you've seen photos of game hunting that link to the De Beers.' Jack helped collect up plates.

'Yes, but game hunting as Bridges just said isn't illegal in Botswana anymore.'

'But it probably was when Marilyn died.' Bridges joined back into the conversation.

'True. So, smuggling ivory taken by the game hunters?' Liz continued.

'Or tiger's balls.' Max pulled his plate back so Jack didn't take it away, obviously still not finished grazing the dip platter.

Liz ignored him, but Max got a snigger from Hemi. 'Smuggling diamonds out of Africa to Australian jewellery manufacturers—is that what we are going with?'

'It's all we've got, but I also need to get a hold of Marilyn's parents. I've only spoken with her sister and I'm still finding it strange I never heard from either Mr or Mrs De Beer after Marilyn's death.'

'I'll ask the Botswana authorises to go out and visit the property. Maybe we can get them to call you to discuss the case here?' Hemi stood up. 'Thanks for the snack Liz, but I've got to get back to relieve my mum's carer.'

'Thanks for rushing over. Let's stay connected guys and if anyone hears from Heather, let us all know.'

'I'm going to head back out to her house, take another look around. I can't think of anywhere else she'll have gone.' Max left his stool out, which Hemi pushed in on his way past, giving Liz a quick wink.

'I'll see if Scott has found anything yet. He seemed to think Heather would be easily tracked.'

'Maybe she's smarter than he thinks.' Jenny moved toward Hemi who wrapped his arm around her shoulder, obviously more comfortable letting everyone know they were an item.

Bridges joined the line of exiting team members. 'Sorry to disturb you on your weekend.' Liz offered as he moved past, then she recalled her earlier unanswered questions. 'I'd say my door is always open if you need to chat about your time in Sydney, but that's not technically true. But I would be happy to listen, if you ever want to share the story.'

Bridges looked like he might say something, then his expression changed and Liz knew today wasn't going to be the day the story was shared. 'Thanks.' He ducked out the door last.

'I thought he was going to spill the beans for a second.' Jack moved toward her.

'Me too. His wife died, didn't she?'

'That's what Jenny said, but that's all we know about him.' Jack wrapped his arms around Liz and she sank into his warm body, the smell of cologne and shampoo mixed with that special scent that was Detective Jack Cunningham.

'Sad. He looks sad.' She looked up at him, feeling guilty that she might finally be getting what she'd always wanted.

'Do we check out the remaining jewellers on our list or are we satisfied *Elegance and Elite* are suspect enough for now?'

'This whole case has my mind running around in circles Jack.'

'Mine too.' Jack held her at arm's length a moment. 'So how about that surfing lesson to take our minds off it?'

'I don't know. I'm really not a water person, unless you count a heated swimming pool.'

'It's fun, besides, ideas pop into my head when I'm not trying to piece evidence and suspects together.'

'Shouldn't we be out looking for Heather?'

'We have done everything we can. Max is doing a double check at her house. We don't know who her friends are. Scott has more chance of tracing her than any of us and he'll call if he finds anything.'

Liz knew Jack was right, but it was so hard to leave something like this unfinished and she wondered why Jack's OCD didn't stretch to his case load. Maybe it did and he was just good at distracting himself. Maybe the surf lesson was a good idea?

'Okay. I'll grab my bathers and get changed.' Jack followed her into her bedroom and stood leaning against the door frame as she pulled her top off and moved toward her expansive walk-in-robe to find her bikini.

'You know,' he moved up behind her as she bent down to open the bottom drawer, 'I could definitely be distracted from surfing for at least an hour or so.' He pressed up behind her and ran his hand over her butt.

'No. If we end up in bed, we'll stay there all day and I've just psyched myself up for this surf lesson, so let's go.'

32

Liz felt like someone had tied her up in a straight-jacket, not that bondage was outside her repertoire, but being wrapped in neoprene from neck to ankle and willingly submitting herself to some form of cold water torture seemed to border on insanity.

'And you do this for fun!' Jack chuckled as he carried a bright blue two inch thick foam surfboard twice Liz's length down from his apartment to the coarse sand of Glenelg Beach.

'It will be worth it. I promise.'

'I've been fed that line before.' Jack ignored the comment and she was glad he had. She really needed to put her brain into gear before speaking, but she couldn't help being a product of her past and he was going to have to learn to deal with what she'd been and who she still was.

The idea that dating a Senior Detective might jeopardise her escort agency wasn't something she wanted to contemplate just yet, so she pushed the thought from her mind as Jack placed the long blue surfboard on the sand alongside his shorter, hard board.

'Okay. Here's your quick lesson in popping up.'

'Popping up?' Liz frowned.

'Don't panic. It's pretty easy once you get the hang of it, but here...' He laid down alongside his board. 'We'll practise it on the beach first.'

'I like that idea.' Liz still wasn't sure water was going to be her happy place. Jack might think the waves were little, but to a five-foot-four weighing in at less than fifty-five kilos she really didn't think any wave was small.

'Lay on your stomach like this.' Liz followed his lead. 'Bend your ankles so only your toes are on the board, up against the raised bit on the deck pad.' He looked at her feet. 'Yep, that's it.' Now you need to push up with your arms like a yoga pose, then lift your butt and push off with your toes bringing one foot up in front of the other.' He demonstrated and Liz shook her head at him, unconvinced.

'Go on. You can do it. You're fit, strong, have good balance. Trust me.' She tried, copying him exactly, but her feet felt like they had a mind of their own. 'Wait up. I think you might be a Goofy Footer.'

'I'm trying.'

'No, it's not a bad thing or anything to do with how good you are at it. Some people lead with their left foot, that's called Natural Footer, some with their right, that's called Goofy.' Liz gave him a look and he grinned in return. 'Trust me. Try popping up with the right foot forward and see if it feels more comfortable.'

Liz laid back down, pushing on her toes and followed the instructions, popping up right foot forward. She smiled, it felt far better.

'Okay, now do it again, this time make sure your front foot lands on this logo, here.' He pointed to the shield shaped logo in black and white placed around the middle of the board. 'That's the balance point of the board. Too far back, the board will slip out from under you. Too far forward and you'll topple over the nose.'

'I'll take your word for it.' Liz tried it again.

'Great, now when you get to your feet, stay in a low crouch and balance your arms out like this.' He demonstrated again.

'Seems like a lot of work.' Liz sighed, but tried again, following the instructions given.

'Excellent. Now let's hit the water.'

'Are you sure? I could drown out there.'

'No way. I'll look after you. Now tie this Velcro leash around your left ankle and we'll get wet.'

'You know, maybe staying in bed was a better version of wet for me after all.'

'I'll do a deal with you. You give me ten waves and if you don't like it by then, we'll head straight back to my place and I'll make sure option 'B' is worth the effort.'

'Option B?'

'The other kind of wet.' His dimple came to life and Liz's stomach fluttered in response. It was well past lunch and Jack always carried an early five-o-clock shadow, one that made him look like a Calvin Klein model in his prime.

'You're on.' Liz grabbed her board and clumsily bolted for the water. Jack came alongside before she reached the water's edge. He waded out, then threw his board onto the surface, Liz followed his lead.

He turned his board around and laid down on it. She copied him. 'Now start paddling.' She did. 'Now, try popping up. The board will wiggle, so don't rush it.' As she pushed up with her hands, the board began to waver, then as she sprang to her feet, it wobbled aggressively and she felt like she was trying to balance on top of a gym ball.

Jack popped up next to her and rode alongside as she tried to scramble to her feet like a cat trying desperately not to get wet. As she finally got her front foot in the right spot, the white water pushed her board forward, toppling her off the side and into the cold water. As her wetsuit became saturated, ice-cold water ran down the inside of the zip line, sending the not so nice kind of shivers throughout her body.

'That was great.' She coughed and spluttered water and rolled her eyes at his enthusiasm.

'I'm not feeling it.' She dragged on her leg rope, towing the board from the wave that was sucking it to shore.

'Nine more to go. We had a deal.' He warned her with a look that said backing out was not an option.

'Okay, nine more.'

****

Liz felt like she'd been run over by a tram as she took the steps, slowly, one foot in front of the other, up to Jack's apartment, but the grin on his face was equally matched by the euphoria she felt over battling her way past ten waves to finally ride all the way to the shore on her feet, without toppling into the white water.

'You were awesome. I knew you'd be good at it.'

'I feel like I've run a marathon.'

'That's just a new lot of muscles learning the ropes. Shower time!' He opened his door and stopped. Liz pulled back, knowing instinctively something wasn't right.

Jack dropped his wetsuit by the door and turned to her, a finger over his lips. She nodded she understood and slipped back against the wall next to the door. Neither of them was armed, but Jack was going to be far more effective on his own, without worrying about her if someone was inside his home.

She watched him disappear, her heart in her mouth, her pulse racing.

'Where the hell have you been?' Liz relaxed at Jack's tone.

'I told Max. Meeting someone.'

'Why not just tell us what was going on? Max has been driving all over town looking for you.'

'And you've been so worried, out surfing.'

'Well there wasn't a lot we could do and worrying wasn't helping anyone. You are such a selfish pain in the arse you know.'

Liz moved inside quickly, her wetsuit dripping a trail from the door. 'Heather. Thank goodness you're okay.'

'At least someone is happy to see me.' Heather looked past Jack, her hands back on her hips. 'I'm not your dog.' Heather's face contorted and Liz knew Jack had hit a nerve. 'Sorry, I wasn't thinking.'

'I needed somewhere safe.'

'You broke in?'

'Not just me.' Jack and Liz were now side by side, both dripping water into a puddle on the white oak laminate floor.

'Who else is here?' He looked around, warily.

'I am.' A heavily accented voice spoke from the hall leading to Jack's room and the bathroom. 'I'm sorry for the invasion of your privacy officer.'

'Detective.' Jack corrected and the African woman nodded.

'I am Taiwo, Detective.'

33

'A call would have been the fucking sensible thing to do.' Max pulled a beer from the carton in Jack's fridge.

'Sorry dad.' Heather joked, but Max wasn't smiling. Jack sat on his small sofa, beer in hand as Liz moved into the living area from the hallway, a towel wrapped around her wet hair.

'I've been out searching high and low for Heather and you two have been surfing. Really! You call *me* irresponsible.'

There was no point trying to defend their actions and Jack wasn't about to try. He'd had a great time with Liz and he wasn't about to apologise for it. For the first time in a long time, he'd been able to really put his case load on hold to focus on enjoying himself.

'Let's go back to the beginning.' Jack got up and moved to the small kitchen. Opening the fridge, he retrieved an open bottle of wine and poured Liz a glass. 'Anyone else?' Heather nodded as he slushed the bottle in the air, Taiwo shook her head.

'I couldn't betray Taiwo's trust. She doesn't know you guys. I've spent the whole day convincing her that she could trust you.'

'That's not the beginning.' Max sounded less agitated.

'Taiwo contacted me about my blog, on Marilyn's cold case. She honestly thought Marilyn was just missing, run away to get out of the crazy mess she'd gotten into.'

'After I spoke with Heather, I was worried Marilyn might be just hiding and Heather investigating, might stir up too much trouble for her. I decided to not answer Heather anymore, to stop her digging deeper.' Taiwo interrupted. 'But when she told me Marilyn was dead, that changed everything.'

'In what way?' Jack held the glass of wine out to Liz, who took it without taking her eyes from Taiwo. Heather got up and moved toward him to retrieve her glass.

'When Marilyn contacted me and asked about why the jeweller was paying her family game reserve, I thought she was going to blow the De Beer's smuggling ring out of the water.'

'So they are smuggling? And you knew about it?'

'Yes, mostly just diamonds now, but it was ivory years ago, lots of it, when governments around the world were putting sanctions on importation, they were smuggling it under the radar.' She took a slow breath in, as if still unsure exactly how much she should share with these strangers.

'Go on.'

'Look, the authorities where I come from are not always truthful.'

'They aren't here either, but you can trust Jack.' Liz took a sip of her wine.

Taiwo studied Jack's face carefully. 'I'm a former escort Taiwo. Believe me when I say you can trust him.'

'The De Beers used Marilyn as an excuse to visit Australia.'

'But they never came to see her.'

'No, but that was always the reason for their visit on immigration paperwork.'

'How do you know so much about the comings and goings of the De Beers?' Max finished his beer, pulled the empty bottle out of the neoprene stubby holder and walked to the kitchen for a refill. 'We should probably get the others here?'

Taiwo tensed.

'Not yet. I've messaged them Heather is okay. That's enough for now.' Jack nodded to the African woman to carry on.

'I'm not sure who has been trying to attack Heather, but I barely made it to the flight out of Botswana alive.'

'How did you get the money?'

'My brother. Not that he knows I used it to fly out of Africa.'

'How does your brother have that sort of money?' Jack knew he was firing questions rapidly, so he took a breath to slow himself down.

'We aren't all poor in South Africa, but money for the aeroplane is a lot detective and you are right to ask why.' She took a moment to compose herself. 'My brother has worked for the De Beer family since we were teenagers. That's one of the reasons I knew Marilyn so well.'

'So he knows all about their smuggling operation?' She nodded. 'And he's been paid well.' Another nod. 'Is he the one chasing Heather?'

'I don't believe so. He wasn't the one trying to kill me when I escaped Botswana but....' She left the rest unsaid.

'But he could be after Heather?' She nodded.

'We'll follow this all up with Anderson and the federal police on Monday. For now, you two are going to have to stay here. Max can't fit you both at his one bedroom flat and going back to your house Heather *isn't* an option.'

Liz looked at him, the thought he had running through his head was written all over her face. There would be no backing up his deal with her tonight.

'You two go back to Liz's place. I'll stay here with these two.' Max hiked a thumb at the two women sitting at Jack's small, round dining table. 'I think I can handle them myself.'

'I couldn't ask you.' Jack started, but Max put his hand up, looking from Jack to Liz, his expression hard to read. Was he glad they were together? Or was it regret in his eyes? Max and Liz were ancient history, but the guy must have still felt something for her. 'You don't have to mate.'

'It makes sense and who wouldn't love a few nights by the beach?' Max grinned.

'Okay. You have my number though. Make sure you check in before lights out tonight.'

'Yes dad.' It was Max's turn to be sarcastic, and this time, he was smiling.

34

Liz rolled over, the warmth of someone in her bed making her disoriented for a moment before her senses smelt the familiar scent.

She looked over. Jack was watching her, his face peaceful. 'What are you looking at?'

'You.' He reached for her, pulling her into his embrace, her head resting on his chest. They snuggled in silence for a minute until Jack spoke again. 'I have to get to work.'

'I know.' She didn't move from his chest. They'd spent the whole weekend together, the first since finally admitting to each other that they had feelings too strong to ignore. From diamond ring shopping, to surfing, to a full day just being together, eating lunch out, making love, eating and making love again, it had been all she'd hoped for.

Now, she was just waiting for the bubble to burst and she wasn't prepared to let him leave to go to work, just yet. He chuckled as she stayed lying on his chest, listening to his heartbeat, her fingers absently winding their way down his abdomen.

'I don't have time to do that justice right now.' He took a hold of her hand, bringing it to his lips and kissing the tips of her fingers, one by one.

'Then stop doing that.' She sat up smiling, before getting out of bed. 'Lots to chase up on today.' She spoke as she moved away from the bed to the bathroom.

'I'll keep you posted, but yeah. I'll see what Anderson can dig up about who the De Beers saw while they were here, where they stayed and hopefully his man in Botswana has managed to visit the game reserve and get some answers.'

Liz moved from the bathroom to her dressing room, picking a pair of lightweight track pants and a sports top, she dressed and returned to the bedroom to find Jack dressed in his suit, ready for work.

'Coffee?'

'Absolutely.' She left the bedroom, Jack trailed behind. 'I need to check and see if we ever got anything from the surveillance cameras near Heather's place. It's been days and I've not heard anything.'

'Who runs through that footage?'

'We need to get a warrant, then we get the recordings from the data company that stores them, then we get Jenny, or Bridges or some other officer to run through it.'

'So if you haven't' heard anything, chances are they found nothing.'

'No, I don't think the recordings have arrived yet.'

'Is that strange?'

'Not unheard of, but it's rare for it to take this long with modern tech. They usually just email it through in a few days.'

'Something else to chase then?'

'Yep. Add it to the list.'

Coffee and breakfast were quick, almost domestic and Liz smiled as Jack gave her a kiss at her door. As she closed it, she resisted the urge to spin around in circles like a giddy teenager, but she did hug herself. The feeling of happiness was shattered as her phone rang.

She checked the caller ID. 'Jenny, what's up?'

'Hemi asked me to call you.'

'That sounds ominous.'

'It is Liz. His contact in Botswana visited the reserve over the weekend and he couldn't get in contact with the De Beers. The only person there was their daughter Tash.'

'Jack said he spoke with her.'

'He did, but that's not the weird bit.'

Liz felt like saying *just get to the point then*, but resisted the urge. Instead, she waited for Jenny to finish.

'He's uncovered a local surveillance file on the De Beer case. We are going to go over it this morning, when Jack gets to work but I think everyone might need to take a look at this.'

'You're sounding deliberately vague Jenny. What's up?'

'The De Beers never left Australia back in two-thousand and nine.' There was a long pause as Jenny gave Liz time to process what she'd just heard.

'Why are we only just finding this out?'

'Because Hemi only checked incoming flight information to begin with, but when he inspected the surveillance file and the cold case information about the De Beer investigation into smuggling, he discovered there was no outgoing flight information.' She took a breath. 'It took him time to get the South African authorities to check their visa and immigration information to see if the De Beers ever made it home.'

'And they didn't.'

'No, they didn't.'

'So we could have two more bodies in that concrete foundation?'

'That or they overstayed their visa.'

'If they did that, they would have had a very good reason for leaving their estate and wealth in South African, untouched for ten years.'

'Exactly.'

35

Jack opened his email, searching for the missing camera footage that should have come through days ago. 'Nothing.'

'What?' Jenny put a coffee down in front of him as he looked up.

'Thanks. I need this one.'

'Early again.' He saw a little twinkle in the corner of her eye and shrugged.

'You can't talk.' She shrugged back before taking a seat opposite him. 'I got your message. Where do we start digging?'

'Anderson is on it for now. It's international anyway. He's got Customs and Immigration involved, let him deal with the red tape.'

'Good call.'

'I called Liz though. Hope you don't mind. We'll need to put our heads together if we are going to close this case.'

'All good. Max texted in this morning that the girls are going okay at my place.' He knew he'd let the cat out of the bag as soon as he'd spoken. There was no hope his partner would miss it.

'So, you did stay with Liz last night.'

'I need you to chase up why we haven't got the footage we needed from outside Heather's house. We'll also call in on Baxter today, and the Excavation company.'

'Change of subject, good dodge there.' Jenny took another sip, but stopped when she saw Jack wasn't playing around anymore. 'On it Boss.' She picked up the desk phone as Jack went back to checking on his emails.

Frustrated there was nothing but more open ends to tie up, he closed the email and sat back, coffee in hand to let his mind mull over all the threads of this investigation. He scanned the whiteboard, before getting up to bring it up to date.

Next to Marilyn's parents' last known date of arrival in Adelaide, he added an arrow to the right and the word *MISSING*. He was just about to add Taiwo's brother when someone called his name.

'Jack.' He turned to see the Chief standing in the doorway by the hall that lead from the Major Crimes office.

'Chief.' The man wiggled a finger for Jack to follow. Jenny lifted an eyebrow as she hung up the phone from chasing down the street camera footage.

'I'll tell you when you get back.' She jotted down notes as Jack made his way out into the hall and up the flight of stairs that lead to the Chief's office.

'What's up?' He entered as the Chief took a seat behind his large timber desk.

'Close the door Jack.'

Jack felt a shiver run down his spine, reminiscent of when the chief had first handed him Marilyn's case. This was going to be personal and in the back of his mind, he had a good idea of what it was about.

'Take a seat.'

'I'm good Chief, make it quick I've got a new lead on Marilyn's case.'

The Chief nodded, then studied his fingertips as they tapped together making a diamond shape, his thumbs continuing to tap. The subject was going to be touchy, just as Jack had expected.

'You're seeing Liz Jeffreys.' It wasn't a question.

'I am. I've been seeing her for a while. We share cases, you know that.'

'That's not what I meant.' The fingers continued to do their dance and Jack swallowed the lump in his throat. Who'd told the Chief they'd been sleeping together? His dad would still have his corrupt finger on the pulse but he couldn't possibly know who he was sleeping with. And if he did, would he want to vandalise his own son's love life?

'Jack. I get it. Liz is a very persuasive woman, but she's the kind of woman you see behind closed doors, not cuddling up in local restaurants.'

They'd had lunch and dinner out yesterday. *Who'd seen them? Had they really been that obvious?* He thought about it a moment, and realised they had. Two lovesick idiots who should have known someone would be watching.

'What I do on my own time is personal Chief. I don't see the issue?'

'You don't see the issue in dating an escort and madam in full public view?'

'She's retired.' The Chief laughed aloud, with enough force to sound like a bark.

'And you think that makes a difference?'

'I don't give a fuck if it does or doesn't.' His adrenalin had kicked in and he knew what the Chief was alluding to, but it didn't matter. He'd resisted his attraction to Liz for too long to go back now.

'I'm just looking out for you Jack. You're on the high road, headed for my job eventually, but women like Lillian Fox don't make Police Chief wives.'

They were all hypocrites. A pretty, sweet wife at home while they fucked the secretary or paid sex workers, all for the right public image, but it was the reference to Lillian's professional name that made Jack's blood run cold.

He knew the Chief had slept with Liz when she was an escort. Half of the notoriety of Adelaide had. Could he live with that? Was her giving up really going to be enough?

'Just take it on advisement Jack. Don't rush off and make a hasty decision, just know that like Max, you can't marry an escort and expect to reach the pinnacle of promotions in the police force.'

Jack was close to throwing his badge at the Chief but he took a slow, measured breath and blew it out equally as slowly. He wasn't rash. He'd never been rash. That's why it had taken him more than six months to tell Liz how he felt. Could he take it back? Did he even want to?

His head hurt as he nodded, turned and left the Chief's office. It took all his self-control not to slam the door on the way out.

As he strode back downstairs and into the Major Crimes office, he felt like his head was about to explode. He must have looked like it, because Jenny's face said she was ready to duck for cover at any moment. She wisely didn't ask questions.

'Report Williams.' Jack spotted Bridges and waved him over from his desk. 'Bridges, you need to hear this.'

The short, bulky guy was all muscle but he moved with speed and grace, which surprised Jack.

'The company who collects and stores the street security camera is privatized, not government. They say the footage was unrecoverable and they apologise for not advising us sooner.'

'Crap.' Jack turned to Bridges, a question on the tip of his tongue but the ex-Sydney sider carried on. 'That's code for someone hacked us or we lost it. It's been wiped.'

'So who do we know that might be able to recover it?' Jenny looked to Jack.

'Scott, but more importantly, who do we know that might have scrubbed it or stolen it?'

'Marshall.' Bridges and Jenny spoke in unison.

'So, is Heather still holding back?' Jack rubbed his temple, his headache growing more intense by the second.

'Not necessarily. She might not know if Marshall took the footage or not. Maybe he didn't tell her. Maybe he liked her and it was his moment of chivalry—find the person who killed her dog and broke into her house.' Jenny was always sharp, able to see from multiple perspectives.

'Maybe. That is another reason for someone to want him dead. Let's call her and find out.'

'No need. When I called Liz this morning, I also called Max. He's bringing them both in to the station shortly.'

'How on earth will he manage to get Taiwo to come in here?'

'He said he had his ways.'

'I hope they don't include hog tying.'

36

Jack opened the door to the glass meeting room at the rear of the Major Crimes office. He watched Taiwo's eyes dart around the room like a skittish thoroughbred, ready to flee at any moment.

'Thanks for coming in Taiwo. I know this must be intimidating.' Jack kept his tone casual and polite.

'Where I come from Detective, the authorities only bring people like me to the station for one reason.'

'Well, this isn't Botswana Taiwo. You're safe with us.' Liz patted put her arm around her shoulder and squeezed for reassurance.

'Heather, if you can sit with Taiwo, we need to run a few things past you both. We seem to be getting even more threads running loose in this investigation and we are struggling to put them all together.' Jack pulled a chair out from the table, and waved Liz to take a seat next to Taiwo. Max sat beside Heather. Jenny stood by the door with Bridges and Jack sat opposite the two women.

'This looks an awful lot like an interrogation Detective. Do we need a lawyer?' Heather drummed her fingers on the table, then sat back and crossed her arms over her chest defensively. 'We are the victims in all of this.'

Until that point, Jack hadn't fully decided if pushing Heather would be needed, but her defensive behaviour told him that that was exactly what he was going to have to do.

'Heather, your friend Marshall,' She fixed her eyes on him, her question unanswered, 'did you know he hacked into the footage from the street cams around your house?' She frowned, the expression hard to read. Was she thinking? Was she stalling?

167

'No. Why would he?'

'Exactly what we wondered, but someone has.' Taiwo squirmed and Jack fixed his eyes on her for a brief moment, before returning his gaze to Heather.

Jenny's mobile buzzed in her pocket, Jack turned at the sound and she nodded before leaving the meeting, her phone already to her ear.

'Taiwo, your brother can't be contacted at the De Beer Resort, or anywhere locally. Do you have any idea where he might be?' Jack watched as she visibly cringed, her hands fidgeting in her lap.

'No,' she finally answered.

'Are you sure?' Jack had a hunch and he was hoping the phone call Jenny just received would confirm his theory.

Jenny re-joined the meeting, nodding the affirmative to his suspicions. This investigation was getting messier with each new piece of evidence they uncovered. So many people working within what? They still didn't know. Diamonds, animal parts smuggling, illegal game hunting, or was it something totally unrelated?

'That isn't exactly true is it Taiwo?' Heather looked to her new friend and the source of all the information she'd used to try and track down Marilyn's disappearance until it had turned into a murder.

'Your brother Kabo flew in on the same flight as you.'

'Taiwo?' Heather was gaping now. It was obvious this had nothing to do with her.

'I didn't see him.' She spoke quickly, wiping her hands down the outside of her long, earthy toned traditional skirt.

'We'll check what seat you both had on the flight. Maybe he followed you, but why would your brother be here, in Adelaide Taiwo? There is still something you aren't telling us.

Did he have anything to do with Heather's attempted abduction?'

'No. He can't have.'

'Why?'

'Because.'

'Because he was with you. Wasn't he?' The woman studied her fingernails, her voice gone. Jack only hoped it wasn't permanent. He knew that having come from a place where police didn't need proof to convict a traditional African woman, meant divulging the truth may be difficult for her.

'It's alright. You've done nothing wrong Taiwo. We just need to get to the bottom of Marilyn and Marshall's murders before someone else gets hurt. Do you know why someone would want to kill Marilyn? Not just a vague idea about diamonds or like you said on the recording, the De Beers being connected. I need something more concrete to gather evidence and put away those who are really guilty.'

'I don't know anything more.' She looked into his eyes, begging him not to push any harder.

'Alright.' He turned to Heather. 'Is there anything you can add before someone else gets hurt? Have you missed out any detail, big or small?' Heather shook her head.

'I've told you everything I know. I started tracking Marilyn's disappearance because Taiwo brought it to my attention. I then got radio silence until Marilyn's remains were found. Now Taiwo is here. That's all I know.'

Jack believed them both, which took him right back to the beginning of his investigation. 'Well, someone thought you knew enough to try and grab you and Marshall's death is most certainly related, but we're missing something, something really important. I can feel it.'

Everyone stared at Jack. Liz and Max had said nothing, just listened. Now as the silence fell on the glass lined meeting room, it was Jenny who broke the tension.

'Boss. We've got interviews to do.' Jack shook himself out of his stupor.

'Yes, Liz, can you have the girls at your place today? I need Max.'

'Sure.' Her quick answer surprised him. 'My place is the gateway hotel these days anyway. Besides, Bennie loves seeing new faces.' She smiled and he let out a breath. It wasn't the answer he'd been expecting. Liz was always so private.

'Max, I need you and Bridges to tag-team on surveillance for us. We've been so focussed on Marilyn's death, we've missed a few things. My fault entirely.'

'Not so Boss.' Jenny offered in defence.

'Either way, we have the construction site where Marshall's body was found. It's time to interview a few people and rattle their cages. The release of the recording didn't cause anyone to bolt, but now that the De Beers have been discovered as never having left Australia, we need to shake something loose.'

Heather and Taiwo exchanged a look that set hairs dancing on Jack's neck. 'What?' He studied them closely.

'Marilyn's parents are still here?' Taiwo's eyes were wide open.

'It appears so, dead or alive we don't know. What is it?'

'It's just.' Heather nodded for Taiwo to go on. Liz put her arm on the African woman's forearm and squeezed.

'It's okay Taiwo. You're safe here.'

'I don't know if it is relevant.' Her accent was so thick Jack had to listen carefully. 'No one has seen the masters of the

Oasis Resort in years. There were rumours. I never worked there, but my brother…'

'Go on.' Jack encouraged.

'My brother said it was a family thing. De Beer seniors had taken a holiday, to let the next generation run the resort.'

'Well, it seems they took a ten-year vacation. Who runs the resort now then?'

'Tash De Beer and her brother, Friedrich.'

'Is either married?'

'I do not know.'

'Williams?'

'On it Boss.' Jenny left the meeting room, heading for her computer, her mobile already back in her hand. Jack knew it would be Anderson that could get that information quickly. They'd have too many hoops to jump through.

'Okay, Liz. Max will drop the three of you at your place, then I'll get him out in the field again.'

Max rolled his eyes. 'Surveillance work. Can't wait.'

'Quit complaining. You love it.'

37

Jack walked up the stairs to the two-storey building on Richmond Road. The company logo featured on a large sign across the façade in less than understated black, gold and green. It looked new and shiny, the name nothing innovative. Just *Baxter Construction and Engineering*.

'These are construction guys Williams, let me do the talking.' Jenny rolled her eyes but said nothing. Jack knew she'd grown up on a farm, but the union types could be hard-nosed chauvinists when they wanted to be.

He walked into the foyer, the commercial carpet squares and fake plants did nothing to soften the feel of the business. No matter which way he looked, hi-vis workwear was everywhere, accompanied by steel-toed work boots and blue or khaki work wear.

The tiny receptionist was the only one in the room who didn't smell of dirt, oil or body odour. Jack took his badge out of his pocket and presented it as he approached the petite blonde with doe like eyes and bright red lipstick.

'I'm Detective Cunningham, this is my partner, Detective Williams. We'd like to see Mr Baxter please.'

'Oh.' She looked around as though she were hoping someone would spring from the dusty plastic palm next to her desk. 'Mr Baxter is busy right now, with a client.'

'We can wait, please let him know we are here though. We'd appreciate it, thanks.' Jack plastered the most reassuring expression on his face and waited patiently as the receptionist took a moment to gather her thoughts.

'Oh.' Again. 'Alright.' She waved them to a dark grey lounge, that looked like it had been passed down by his grandfather, before picking up the phone on her desk. 'I know Sir. Sorry it's just...' She stopped, listened, nodded and waited. 'A Detective is here Sir?' She rushed the words into the only gap her boss seemed to give her.

More silence from the reception made it clear she was getting specific instructions from her employer and her face said she didn't like them one little bit. 'Yes Sir.' She put the phone back into the handset cradle and looked up at Jack, plastering a smile on her dial like she'd just entered a Miss Congeniality contest.

'Mr Baxter will be tied up all day and he won't be able to see you Detectives. I'm very sorry.'

'We can come back with a warrant.' The smile slipped from her face like a landslide as her colour went pasty white.

'Can I help?' A tall man with a perfect man-scape, wearing a tailored suit approached the reception desk where Jack now stood, looming over the receptionist. His face smiled, but his eyes drilled into Jack's. The suit, the posture, it all looked out of place amongst the workwear and basic furnishings.

Jack pulled his badge out. 'I'm Detective Cunningham and this is Detective Williams.' His eyes stayed on Jack's.

'How can I help?' That smarmy smile again.

'We'd like to speak with Mr Baxter, about the homicide victim that was discovered Friday at his construction site.'

'Which site would that be?' Not a flicker at the word *homicide*. 'Mr Baxter has 'bout a dozen projects on the go at the moment.' Jack could hear an accent, but his mind was having difficulty focussing on the origin.

'The one on Main South Road near the new overpass. Where I'm sure you've heard a homicide victim was found.' Still not a flinch.

Jack watched Williams out the corner of his eye as he spoke. He could see her hackles were up. The man in front of him hadn't yet bothered to acknowledge her presence. That was good in Jack's book. It gave her a chance to observe what else was happening around them.

He raised an eyebrow at his partner, indicating she should look around. She nodded before turning to take in the rest of the office area.

'Yes, of course.' There was something in the accent that was tickling the back of Jack's mind, but he wasn't sure what.

'Who are you anyway? I don't see why I'm speaking with you and not Mr Baxter.' Jack looked closely at the man's expression. Lawyer, executive maybe? He had his money on lawyer.

'*Howzit* you need to speak to Mr Baxter? I'm sure I can answer your questions or the site manager can.'

Jack's eyebrows rose as the man's accent finally made sense. He'd done very well to keep it hidden. Maybe he'd lived in Australia a long time, but there was no doubt in Jack's mind now that he needed to dig into Mr Baxter's background and find out who this guy was too.

'We spoke with the manager on site Friday. He said that Mr Baxter was the first to know about the demolition due for today.'

'He would be. He runs the company.'

'Really. Isn't that something a middle manager might handle?' Jack made a show of looking around. 'This business looks like a pretty big operation. Surely the owner doesn't spend too much time hands-on when it comes to day to day operations. He'd have people for that, right?'

The man shrugged. 'I think it might be time to leave Detective. I'm sure if you make an appointment, and bring a warrant, we can arrange for Mr Baxter to meet with you.'

'No need. I think we have *all* we need for now.' The man looked surprised, but wiped the expression away quickly. Jack could see he was mulling over everything he'd said to decide what he might have given away.

'Williams. Let's go.' He beckoned Jenny who was over the far side of the office area speaking with a small group of workmen. She looked up, gave one of them a card and jogged to catch Jack as he headed out the double glass doors.

38

'You gave up easily.' Jenny caught up to Jack.

'Not really. We weren't getting anything without a warrant. That guy who spoke to us.' Jenny looked at him, her brows knitted together. 'He's a Saffa.'

'A what?'

'South African. I couldn't place the accent at first, very well hidden, only a couple of words made me think he even had an accent, but when he said *Howzit,* instead of how's that, I knew.'

'So you think he or the firm are connected to Marilyn's death? That's a big leap Boss. There has to be a few thousand ex-South Africans in Australia.'

'Yes, but I don't believe in coincidences Williams. What did the construction workers have to say?'

'Seems Baxter has been very aloof. One of the guys I spoke to has been with the company for twenty years. Baxter used to put on a Christmas do every year. Hasn't done it in years.'

'How many years Williams?' Jack's stomach was rolling around doing summersaults as Jenny grinned like the cat that ate the canary.

'Guess?'

'Not in the mood, but if I had to, I'd say ten years. Sound about right?'

'Exactly. I gave him my card and asked him to let me know if anything weird happens.'

'Weirder than a missing boss and a dead hacker? We need to interview the site manager again. Find his address from the list of names he gave you.'

Jack opened the door of his old BMW as Jenny got in the passenger's side, phone already in hand, finger scrolling through the details.

'I've got his number here. We should call him because he'll be on site somewhere.'

'Try him now then. I need to call Anderson and get him to check on a few things for me.'

'Okay.' Jenny looked disappointed the calls weren't the other way around, but Jack really needed to make sure Anderson dug deep.

He pulled his old flip phone out of his jacket pocket and pressed speed dial for the Federal Police officer. It rang twice before Hemi picked up.

'Bro. What's up?'

'Sorry to keep calling for work mate. We should catch up for drinks and a meal soon. Sorry Sunday got messed up by this case.'

'It's pretty standard stuff in our line of work hey. All good. What can I do for you?'

'We just went to see the owner of the construction company who managed the site Marshall's body was found at. Something funky is going on mate.'

'In what way?'

'Baxter, the owner, hasn't been seen in years, like ten years.' Hemi whistled. 'And the guy who played defence in the office, all smarm and no charm, had a South African accent.'

'And you think things are connected?'

'Call it a gut feeling mate, but this guy was stonewalling. He's definitely a Saffa and the site manager put us on to Baxter, so he either did it to draw attention away from himself, or he did it because he's in deep and wants out. Maybe he's the one who dropped the diamond photo file on site too.'

'So what do you want from me?'

'I need you to run the names of all employees at Baxter's business and see if you can find this Saffa guy. He might be a lawyer, who works for the firm. See what you can find. I wouldn't ask you, he's likely not even an Australian citizen, so my search parameters will be restricted.

I'm going to pull driver's license photos of Baxter from the last decade or so and see if we can get a glimpse of who is playing at being Baxter or if Baxter is even coming in to work at all. The receptionist knew something. I think I'll get Jenny or Liz to try and talk with her outside the office.'

'It's all go with you bro. I'll get on to it now. See if immigration has anything on the guy, if I can get a photo of him. Can you give me a description?'

'I'll text some details through. If you get any mug shots, I'll be able to identify him.'

'Leave it with me.'

'Thanks mate.' Jack hung up, put his phone in his pocket and started the car engine.

'Where to?' he asked Jenny as he pulled the car away from the curb heading east on Richmond Road.

'He's not answering Jack.'

'That's pretty strange. A site manager, not answering his phone.'

'Exactly what I was thinking.'

'Where does he live?'

Jenny scrolled on her phone again. Jack carried on down the road, waiting for directions. 'Morphett Vale. Just off Flaxmill Road.'

'Okay. I'll take a left down Marion Road. Just update Max and Bridges on what's happening.'

'On it.' Jenny dialled Max's number and put the phone on speaker. 'Technology hey.' She smiled.

'Smart Arse.'

'I know.' Max answered and Jenny chuckled. 'What's happening?'

'I've asked Anderson to run a few things for me. We got nowhere interviewing Baxter. He might not even be alive for all we know. We were intercepted by a South African, lawyer looking guy. Can you head over to follow the guy if he leaves? I'll send a description, but I don't think you'll miss him.'

'Sure. Nothing's happening with the excavation guys. They've been on another site all morning since I followed them out of the depot at six. I spoke with a few onsite and nothing seems out of whack.'

'Good. It was a long shot anyway. They knew about the demolition order but we've not been able to connect them to Marilyn, Marshall or the De Beers.'

'Have we found anything more about where the De Beers stayed while they were here?'

'Bridges has been checking out a few addresses Anderson gave us. Nothing he's called about. I'm just about to let him know where we are at. I'll update you if anything pops.'

'All good. Stay safe mate. This one is getting murkier by the minute.'

'Will do.' Jack nodded and Jenny hit the end call button. 'Text Max the details, we'll call Bridges after we speak with the site manager.' Jack pulled his car onto Flaxmill Road. 'Where to?'

'Just take the third left.' Jack got into the left lane and took the third as instructed. 'Now a right.' He obliged. 'Should be the house just up here.'

As they approached, Jack could see too many cars lining the road for a suburban street and smoke was billowing up into the sky. They passed three press vans representing all the major stations. The blaze was almost extinguished, but four fire units were on scene, along with an ambulance.

Jack pulled his car to the curb and turned off the engine as a uniformed officer approached the vehicle. 'I'm sorry, I'm going to have to ask you to clear the area.' Jack pulled his badge out of his pocket without a word.

The officer nodded and ushered him through. 'I didn't realise anyone called you in Sir.'

'We were already on our way Constable.' The young officer nodded. 'Get some crime scene tape up Constable.'

'Sir?' Jack knew why he was unsure. It was just a fire. Houses burnt down every week. Why was this one special?

'It's a possible arson, possible homicide scene now.' The Constable didn't ask any more questions. Instead, he called out to two other officers and got to doing his job as quickly as possible. 'Get these bystanders further back too.' The Constable nodded.

'Curiouser and curiouser.' Jenny joked quietly as they approached the Fire Chief.

'You got that right.'

39

Jack didn't need to show his badge to the Fire Chief. 'I'll need arson on this Frank.'

'You got it Jack. I was already thinking of calling them in. The point of origin looked a bit off.'

'In what way?'

'House fires usually start inside, near a heater or candle, maybe even a faulty appliance in the kitchen, but this looks like it started at the back of the house. That's where it was burning the hottest when we got here.'

'And that's unusual?' Jack followed the Fire Chief down the side driveway, the smell of wet smouldering wood filled his nostrils but what couldn't be mistaken was the scent of burnt flesh. It wasn't the kind of smell that ever left you once you'd breathed it in and Jack knew it only too well.

They both stood in the backyard, facing the long back veranda, the mist of cooling debris rising into the air.

'This one looks like it started outside, here on the back veranda. We've got this pile of crap in front of the back door and I'm sure there was accelerant. You can see the speed of that burn trail there, up the wall.'

Jack stood back from the rickety structure. Although the fire was mostly out, the radiated heat from the smouldering building materials prevented him from drawing any closer, but he could see what Frank was talking about.

Innersprings coiled in all directions, distorted by the intense heat and there was what looked like an old outdoor umbrella pole and other items that simply didn't belong shoved up against the old nineteen-fifties screen door.

'I'll wait for the report Frank, thanks. Do we know if the guy lived alone?'

'Not sure Jack. We've not been able to get inside. It's not secure yet. I'll send a recovery team in once we get it cooled down enough and make sure nothing is going to cave in on them. You'll be the first to know how many victims we've got.'

'Thanks Frank.' Jack walked down the driveway. The grass between the two lines of concrete that marked the vehicle tracks was scorched, the ash rose with each footfall.

'What next?' Jenny asked as he returned to his car.

'We canvas the neighbours. See who's been in the area. Anything strange, any unusual vehicles. You know the drill. I'll get Bridges out here now.'

****

Jack's feet ached. He'd stood around for over an hour waiting for the fire fighters to give clearance for police forensics and the arson unit to attend the scene. Half of him wanted to leave and follow up other leads, but his gut was telling him that this fire, and the site manager's possible murder could be the key to unravelling the case, so he'd stayed until the body could be recovered.

Jenny approached as forensic officer Penny got out of her van, retrieving two large boxes that looked like toolboxes. The two women waved at one another, exchanged a quick greeting before Jenny stopped in front of Jack.

'You and Bridges finish up here. I'll see what Penny can tell us. Then I'll head back and put a rocket up Doc's butt. We need to confirm ID on this guy.'

'Good luck speeding Doc up. You know how methodical he is.' Jack didn't smile and Jenny moved back to continue canvassing witnesses with Bridges.

Penny walked past on her way to the burnt-out front doorway. 'There isn't going to be much evidence left in there Jack.'

Jack followed her inside, the smell of ash wasn't enough to drown out the sweet, sickly smell of burnt flesh. 'Anything you can tell us could help Penny.'

'You know we can't confirm anything until we've run forensics.'

'I know, but maybe we can confirm forced entry.' Jack stopped to study the door jamb. It was nothing more than a charred remnant. The lock melted like it had been through a blacksmith's forge.

'Not much chance of that.' Penny snapped a few photos before dropping her camera around her neck and continuing into the building.

'Hey Mike. We good to go all the way in?' she asked a fireman who nodded.

'All good Penny. We've secured the place.'

'Thanks.' She ducked under a charred, fallen rafter as they both gingerly moved through the shell of a burnt-out hallway.

'He's in the lounge room on the right,' the fireman called as he moved out of the building.

Penny didn't respond, the smell was enough to lead a blind man. 'Here he is.' Penny put her bags down and opened the first one which pivoted open like Jack's fishing tackle box.

'Doc on his way?'

'Yep. He'll be about ten minutes.'

'He didn't try and flee the fire.'

'Maybe the smoke alarm didn't wake him, drunk perhaps.' Penny picked up what was once a scotch or bourbon bottle to make her point.

'Okay. I'll leave you both to it. If you find anything out of the ordinary, let me know.'

'Will do Jack.' Penny didn't look up, she was already snapping photos of the victim and Jack didn't need to hang around and watch. The sight of the skull was enough for him, the burnt flesh pulled back from exploded eyeballs, the lips shrivelled away to reveal white teeth that looked like something from a horror movie against the blackened flesh.

As Jack got into his car, his phone rang. He looked at the caller ID and answered.

'What's up Max?'

'Our boy is on the move. I'll let you know where we end up.'

'Be safe Max. We've got three maybe more already dead.'

'Three?'

'Yeah, our site manager has been fried.'

'Okay, I'll be careful mate. I'm just gonna take a few photos.'

40

Jack stood at the coffee cart outside the office and waited, his mind drifting as he mulled over the case.

'Coffee's up Jack.'

'Thanks mate.' Jack took the tray from the barista, chuckling at how he'd managed to convert Bridges to a reusable cup, something he'd never managed to do with Max.

'Hey Jack.'

Jack turned to see Hemi strolling up alongside. 'I need to talk with you. Got a sec?'

'Sure. You want a coffee?'

'No I'm good bro.' Jack watched Hemi's expression closely. The guy looked like his dog had just died and Jack had a sinking feeling.

'What's up?' Jack moved inside the foyer and pressed the elevator call button.

'Nothing good.'

'Let me get these coffees to the team before you throw any bad news our way.'

'Good idea.' The elevator doors opened and Jack stepped in. Hemi pressed the third-floor button and they both rode up in silence. Jack could see the news wasn't going to be good and his adrenalin was already spiking. This was going to be a jurisdiction thing; he could feel it in his bones.

The elevator doors opened and Hemi held them open as Jack exited first.

Jenny looked up as they approached, her usual smile over caramel coffee was nothing on her expression when she saw Hemi behind Jack.

'Kia Ora crew.' There was no cheer in Hemi's signature greeting.

'Anderson.' Bridges nodded as Jack put a coffee down on his desk.

'Hey.'

'What brings you in here?' Jenny asked casually.

'Bad news. Sorry. I was running that Saffa search on the guy from Baxter's construction business and alarm bells sounded when I got close to finding his name in the system.'

'Feds are on him already?' Jack sipped his coffee from the edge of his desk. Somehow, he didn't feel like sitting down in his chair.

'Looks that way.'

'I thought the case on the De Beers was shelved years back?'

'It was. This guy has a file all of his own, but I can't tell you any more than that.'

'So are you in on the federal investigation Anderson?'

'Nah bro. This is above my pay grade.'

'Didn't think that was possible.'

'Neither did I, but I've been locked out.'

'So what do we do now?' Jenny looked from Anderson to Jack and back.

'We keep on our investigation; we just give this guy a wide birth.' Jack looked at Anderson for confirmation.

'Yes and no.' Hemi looked uncomfortable.

'What does that mean?'

'Look Jack. Anything that links to our guy, can't be pursued. It could bust open a federal case and stuff up years of surveillance.'

'We've got three dead and all roads could lead to Saffa boy. I can't guarantee our paths won't cross Anderson.'

The big Kiwi took a long, slow breath. 'Just be careful bro. I'm not even privy enough to know if this guy is the bad guy, the undercover guy or the whistle blower. He could be anything to this investigation.'

'He's no whistle blower. Take my word for it. His eyes say he's more likely a trained killer. Undercover maybe, but then he'll have nothing to worry about. I won't be aiming for him if he didn't pull any triggers.'

'Well, you've been officially cautioned bro. That's all I've been told to do.'

'Consider your job done then mate.' Jack's tone was far from casual, making it clear to Anderson, there'd be no calling him off.

'See you all later.' He turned on his heel and left the office.

41

Max ignored his rumbling stomach, his eyes were focussed on the old warehouse tucked away in the back streets of Port Adelaide. Missing lunch was nothing new to him, but not having a smoke to help pass the boredom was still foreign.

He reached into his glove box and pulled out the almost forgotten packet of nicotine gum. Popping one out he placed it in his mouth, under his tongue and waited for it to soften. Chewing the stuff was borderline foul so he let the nicotine absorb without biting down.

The tall man in the expensive suit had disappeared inside a few hours ago. No one else had left the construction company office with him and no one else had entered the warehouse since. Max sat, waiting, his camera on the passenger seat alongside him, ready to shoot when needed.

The sound of a vehicle made him turn around. From his position across from the warehouse, tucked down an alley, he could see a black van pulling up outside. The tall roller door opened slowly, revealing a poorly lit interior with rows of pallet-racking lining each wall. Some full, some almost bare.

Max reached for his camera, snapping a dozen photos as the van pulled inside. His mark stood just inside the door, another rough looking guy tapped the driver's window which wound down a moment before carrying on inside the warehouse.

The doors slowly lowered and Max snapped more shots until the door hit the bottom and he pulled his camera away from his eye, just in time to see something coming at him from his right.

He wasn't quick enough. His door was opened and two men in dark blue overalls, balaclavas and utility vests loaded with spare ammunition dragged him out from behind the wheel. Before he could reach his gun, they'd pulled it from the holster and shoved him up against the wall, out of view of the warehouse.

'What the fuck are you doing?' the officer on his right spoke quietly into his ear.

Max's face was pressed so hard up against the old red brick building that he could barely articulate words.

'I'm a PI. My badge is in my back pocket.'

Hands patted his butt, retrieving his wallet and opening it to reveal his ID. 'You're in the wrong place mate. This is a police investigation.'

'I know it is. I'm consulting with the police.'

'Federal?'

'No mate. Local. Major Crimes.'

'You need to check in with your boss then because this case is out of local jurisdiction.'

Max kept his hands up as the men let him move back from the wall. 'First I've heard of it. We're working on multiple homicides.'

'Just get in your car and move on or we'll arrest you for obstruction.'

'All good mate. No need to get your knickers in a knot.' Max moved back to the driver's side of his car and slid in behind the wheel. The two officers stood back, automatic weapons held tight to their chests as they waited for him to start the engine and drive away.

His heart was still pounding as he turned right and moved away from the warehouse. He hit Jack's number on his hands-free display, fingers shaking.

'I just got my arse handed to me in a sling mate.'

'You okay?'

'Yeah, but the Feds just sent me home with a kick up the arse. What's going on?'

'Seems we've stumbled into a Federal surveillance operation.'

'I don't know Jack. These two guys were from Special Forces Unit. Like Anderson's team. All done up to the nines in their pretty blue jumpsuits and balaclavas.

'Get back here mate. We'll touch base with Liz and put our heads together. It's going to have to be softly, softly, if we want to stay on this case.'

'You got it. See you in twenty.'

****

Liz stood in front of the whiteboard, her hands on her hips. Jack couldn't help but smile behind her back.

'Are Taiwo and Heather settled?' Jack handed Liz a cappuccino.

'Bennie will keep an eye on them and let me know if they go anywhere, plus, Scott contacted me this morning after you...' She saw Bridges and Jenny listening and let the rest of her sentence hang a moment. 'He's been tracking Heather's digital trail from when she took off to meet Taiwo without telling us.'

'Is that legal?' Jenny moved closer to the whiteboard, a red marker in hand. She added another photo to the two victims in the middle of the whiteboard. Len Montgomery, forty-two, divorced and had worked for Baxter's construction company for the past ten years.

'For you no, for me, it's a grey area.' Liz shrugged and Jenny carried on writing details on the whiteboard.

'Go on.' Jack gave Jenny the *don't interrupt* look and the junior detective skulked.

'He said someone else is monitoring Heather's digital footprint. So far he hasn't worked out who or where the tracking is coming from.'

'That's not good. We really shouldn't leave them alone if that's the case.'

'I'll send Max over when he gets here.'

'Over where.' Max moved up behind them to see why they were all huddled around the whiteboard.

'You move pretty stealthily for a big guy you know.' Liz spun around. 'Scott said someone is trailing Heather's digital communications, emails, her regular phone.'

'So they'll know where she is?'

'Possibly, but my building security is tighter than the Australian Mint. Bennie is also keeping a close eye on things.'

'And Bennie will be a lot of good. He's older than Jack's dad. Plus, you've already had a break-in there before. I'll head over in a minute and check on them.'

'What about those guys that jumped you?' Jack returned to his desk, the whiteboard forgotten.

'Who jumped you?' Liz looked outraged. 'Are you okay?'

'I'm touched by your concern.' Max grinned. 'I'm fine. They said they were Federal Police.'

'Did they show you any ID?'

'No.' Max rubbed his chin. 'I was a little frazzled, have to admit. Didn't even think of it.'

'So they could have been involved? Which means they would know you've been watching the warehouse.' Liz sat on the corner of Jack's desk, cappuccino still in hand.

'Jenny, call Anderson. Ask him for one more favour if he can. Check and see if AFP have a special unit on surveillance at the warehouse. Max, give her the address.'

'Forty-Nine Lipson Street.' Jenny wrote it on the board as Max spoke, next to the word Saffa, with a line going up to Len's photo.

'I'll call him now.' She tossed the red marker onto her desk as she moved past, her mobile phone already in her hand as she headed out into the hall for some privacy.

'So what's going on?' Max looked from face to face until someone looked like they'd explain.

'The Feds *are* watching the construction company and in particular our Saffa friend, but Anderson couldn't tell us more than that. He said we couldn't move against the guy, it could stuff up years of surveillance and undercover work.'

'That's bullshit. We've got dead people. Homicide trumps bloody smuggling or drugs or anything else.' Max looked at Bridges who shrugged as if to say *don't ask me.*

'We all know Federal trumps us all anytime it wants Max. We're not giving up just yet. I've got an autopsy to attend. The site manager, Len Montgomery has coincidentally worked at Baxter's since Mr Baxter himself disappeared from public life. Max, you check on the girls at Liz's place. Bridges, you run some things through the motor vehicle registration office.'

Bridges got a pen out of his jacket pocket and pulled a pad of paper across his desk. 'What am I looking for?'

'While you're there, I've got surveillance photos of a black van entering the warehouse.' Max pulled the camera strap off from around his neck and opened the card slot.

'Ok. Track that, then I want driver's licence photos of Baxter from fifteen years ago, then see if you can find a current one.'

'Okay. Anything else?'

'Actually yeah, the registration for the van that was used to try and grab Heather, it was stolen, right?'

'It was.'

'Any idea what address it was stolen from?'

'Give me a second.' Bridges tapped at keys and Jack couldn't help but notice he was a hunt and peck kind of guy. The wait was excruciating. 'It was stolen from the Noarlunga Railway Station carpark. Owner said she got off the train, went to go to her car and it wasn't where she left it.'

'That's close to Morphett Vale.'

'What are you thinking?' Liz asked as she put her finished cup down on Jack's desk.

'Did we check CCTV footage for the station?'

'We did, but the woman parked too far away.'

'That's very close to Montgomery's place, which was just torched. Looks like our Saffa friend could be cleaning house.'

Jenny walked back into the room and all eyes fell on her. Her face gave away the answer to their question without it being asked.

'There's no Special Forces police unit on Saffa guy that Anderson knows about.'

'Shit! That was a dumb-arse move on my part.'

'Not really Max.' Jack stood and patted his ex-partner on the back. 'I'd rather have you in one piece and if you'd pushed it, you might not be.'

'True.' Max nodded, reassuring himself.

'There's more. The Saffa guy in the suit from Baxter's finally has a name, Johan Kruger.' Jenny grinned sheepishly.

'Nice work. How'd you get Anderson to cough that up?' Max handed the memory card to Bridges as he waited for an answer that wasn't going to come.

Liz rolled her eyes at him and he frowned. 'What?'

'If you don't know I'm not going to point it out to you.' Liz turned to Jack. 'What next?'

'Williams and I'll go over to the morgue and see if we can sit in on Montgomery's autopsy. Hopefully we can get enough from the body to start pulling warrants and organising searches. Bridges, while you're running details, get any known associates of Montgomery. I've got a feeling we'll need them.'

'Will do.'

'What are you planning Liz? Head back with Max and babysit Goth girl and our African friend?' Jack opened his drawer and retrieved his gun, checking the safety before placing it in his shoulder holster and closing the drawer.

'Anderson said that a few names on that list Bridges gave him, including *Guild and Glover* staff popped up as having travelled to South Africa, so I need to quiz Robert Glover about those trips. Then there's Gregory and Robert's business partner. South Africa is a strange destination for so many staff from the same company to be traveling to.'

'I agree. Be careful though. So far, Mr Glover has been very cooperative, but we have to remember all three jewellers were his clients and Gregory was very evasive.' Jack looked at Jenny. 'Grab your gear. Do you need a lift?' he asked Liz.

'No. I'll take a taxi.'

'All good. See you...later.' Liz smiled and Jenny's eyebrows rose from across the desk as she leant into her drawer to retrieve her weapon.

'Don't say a word.' Liz warned and Jenny chuckled.

'Got the info on that van. Do you want me to follow up?'

'Run the dead manager's connections first. Then see if anything links the site manager to the van that grabbed Heather or this black van at the warehouse.'

'Okay, I'll call once I get all the info.'

42

The attractive blonde receptionist sat at the desk outside the morgue entrance. She smiled and fluttered her eyelashes but Jack was too focussed on getting to Doc Holbrook to notice.

'You better tell her you're off the market,' Jenny whispered with a nod as they moved past.

'Doc is ready for you Jack.' She hadn't heard Jenny, but Jack had and he wasn't gracing his junior partner with an answer.

They moved on down the hall, through the thick plastic curtain. The temperature dropped another ten degrees.

'You ready for this?' Jack looked at Jenny, his hand on the autopsy suite door. His partner had seen plenty of dead bodies in her time as a constable in the bush and now as a detective, but she'd only been on morgue duty a few times and burn victims were never easy to take.

Jenny took a long slow breath and nodded. 'Can't be worse than decomp, right?' Jack didn't know how to answer that. Decomp was rough on the nasal passages that was for sure, but burnt bodies were extra unpleasant. The body contorted as fire consumed the muscles, shortening them and making the victim shrink into an almost foetal position.

He pushed the door open. 'Hey Doc.'

'Hey yourself detectives.' Doctor Holbrook was a seasoned pathologist who knew his way around a police autopsy. Every scrap of evidence the body could furnish, Doc would find.

'Thanks for fitting this one in for us Doc. It's linked to two other homicides.' He and Jenny moved closer, but Jack noticed Jenny hung back a little.

'I hear one of those is Marilyn De Beer. It's the least I could do Jack.'

'Anything stand out yet?'

'He looks like a mummy from the Cairo museum.' Jenny commented, moving closer now.

Doc turned to the younger detective, happy to offer an explanation. 'It happens as the body dehydrates in mummies, in severe burn victims, they lose a lot of moisture very quickly and the muscles and tendons shrink. It has a similar appearance, often resulting in the victim assuming what we often call the pugilistic position or boxer position.' He mimicked the hands raised in defence.

Without missing a beat, Doc turned to Jack to offer an answer. 'I'll need to clean the bones first, but look at this.' Doc pulled back tortured and burnt skin to reveal what looked like a hole in the victim's skull. 'Look familiar?' He looked from the wound to Jack's eyes and back.

'Blunt force trauma. Same weapon?'

'I can't be sure. I'll take photos, blow up the images, clean the bones and see if there's any imprint, but position, depth, dimension, are all similar.'

'So he was dead before the fire?'

'Unconscious definitely, dead, most likely, considering the size and severity of this wound.'

'That's one small mercy I guess.'

'That's only the tip of the iceberg I'm afraid. He has fractured phalanges on both hands.'

'Torture?'

'That's my early appraisal. Once again, I'll need to clean the bones, confirm the fractures haven't begun to mend, but I think this guy was tortured before he was struck on the head and burned.'

'Nasty.' Jack saw Jenny resisting the urge to hold her nose, instead she practised the technique he'd taught her on her first decomp case—breath through the mouth, not the nose.

'One more thing Jack, when I did the x-ray, and found the fractures, I also found this.' Doc Holbrook pulled a film from an envelope on the bench and placed it over the illuminator on the side wall. The image was of the victim's shoulder. There were no breaks, but Jack could see instantly what the Doc had found.

'A bullet?'

'Most definitely. I'll do ballistics once I get it out. A recent injury, but long enough ago to show signs of healing.'

'I think I might be able to supply you with a ballistics match on that one.'

Doc lifted an eyebrow and waited for an explanation.

'Max shot and hit a would-be kidnapper last week. I think this might just be our man. I noticed he looked tender in the left shoulder Friday on site, but didn't think much about it. This makes a lot of sense.'

'Glad I could help.'

'Thanks Doc, send the full report as soon as you can and I'll get Max to drop by so Penny can test his gun for a ballistics match.'

'I hope he filed a report.' Doc called over his shoulder as they left the autopsy suite.

'You know paperwork has never been his strong point Doc.'

'Don't I know it.' Jack could see Doc chuckling as he turned to leave.

43

Jack pulled his flip phone out of his pocket and pressed Max's speed dial number. They'd worked together for years, and number *One* was still reserved for Max.

'Max. We need to match your gun with a bullet in our arson victim's shoulder.'

'Hi Jack, yep, I'm fine thanks mate.' Max sounded amused.

'Sorry mate. This case is making me feel like I'm running around in a hamster-wheel that won't stop.'

'I know what you mean. What do you need?'

'Your gun, to Penny for a ballistics test A.S.A.P.'

'You got it. Anything else?'

'You bored baby-sitting already?'

'I feel a bit caged in Liz's fancy digs with these two. Let me know if you find anything worth me following up. I'll get my gun to Penny as soon as Liz is back.'

Jack heard Heather complaining about not needing a nursemaid in the background. 'I'll keep you posted.' Jack hung up. 'Let's get back to see if Bridges has dug up anything useful yet.'

****

Liz smiled at Stephanie as she walked across the highly-polished tile floor and stopped by the counter. 'Is Robert free?'

'Sorry Ms Jeffreys.' All formality, no hint of their connection. The girl was smart. 'He's not available at the moment. He called in sick.'

'Is that normal?' Liz raised an eyebrow.

'Mr Gregory is available, if this is about your accounts?'

'Fine.' She thought that could work out better. After years of working as an escort, she was good at reading people and her instincts told her Robert had nothing to do with Marilyn's death, but the link to some of the firm's accounts and South Africa was real.

'Take a seat, I'll give him a call.' She smiled sweetly and Liz nodded, moving away to sit on the edge of a large tweed sofa—one of many spread out around the expansive foyer.

A few moments passed and Liz resisted the urge to check her emails or scroll through the internet, instead she reached for a Vogue magazine and thumbed through it without taking any real notice of what the latest trends in interior design might be.

She noticed the man before he approached. Jack had given a less than flattering description, but Liz was mildly impressed. The older man was in his late fifties, to early sixties, lean and dressed impeccably. But that was where the admiration stopped. He walked with an arrogant stride, his hips thrust out, his shoulders back. The fake tan wasn't something she was unfamiliar with, but the man's white smile felt forced and the lines at the edges of his eyes said he was mildly anxious about seeing her.

'Ms Jeffreys, we are still getting all your paperwork over from your previous accountant so I'm not exactly up to speed with your account yet.'

'No problem Mr Gregory, I'm just checking in and was hoping to see Robert, but since he isn't here, I think I can probably get the information I need from you instead.'

He grimaced ever so slightly but Liz didn't miss it. 'Come through to my office then.'

Something about Gregory was tickling her senses and she couldn't be sure if it was him, his mannerisms or the vibe, but if she'd possessed Spiderman's famous Spidey senses, they'd have been setting off alarm bells in that moment.

'Did you work with Marilyn De Beer at all Mr Gregory?' The accountant coughed but recovered quickly, the fake smile back in place.

She knew she was going straight to the point. Tact had never been her strong point but beating about the bush just wasted valuable time. Heather was stuck in her house and the quicker she solved the case, the quicker she could get the young woman home to her own house and get her own space back to be with Jack.

'I thought you were here about your accounts Ms Jeffreys.'

'Did I say that?' She waited, knowing she'd not mentioned her accounts, only that she wanted to see Robert. 'Do you know where Robert Glover is Mr Gregory?'

'He's called in sick today Ms Jeffreys.'

'I've known Robert Glover for over twenty-five years Mr Gregory. He's not the type to take a sick day, even if it is a Monday.' Gregory's eyebrows pressed together a moment.

'Maybe it was a personal matter.' He waved his hand. 'None of my business. I'm just an associate.'

'You didn't answer my question.'

'Ms De Beer. Yes, I worked with her.'

'Do you handle the accounts of *Elegant and Elite*, *Mills and Burns*, and *The Diamond House*?' If he was involved, he did well not to show it.

'I'm not familiar with those accounts and even if I was, I wouldn't be discussing them with another client Ms Jeffreys. I'm sure you understand. Our client confidentiality is extremely import.' The smarmy smile returned.

'Of course. Ever been to South Africa?' That got a response. Gregory sat back in his chair, his arms crossed over his chest, but he removed them almost immediately.

'Not sure of the reference Ms Jeffreys.'

The picture of the game hunter, with the lion came to her. Now she understood the tingling in the back of her mind. 'I've seen an old photo from the Oasis Game Reserve. You've known the De Beers a long-time Mr Gregory.' It wasn't a question.

He coughed, pushed his chair back as he scratched the back of his ear, a tell she hadn't seen yet. She had him rattled.

'I think I'll get your accounts together, so I'm up to speed on *your background* before I call you in for an appointment Ms Jeffreys.'

Was that a threat? It felt a lot like a threat, the words, the body language, the tone of voice.

'That won't be necessary Mr Gregory. I'll deal only with Robert in the future.' Liz stood, turned and moved toward the door.

'Ms Jeffreys.' Liz turned around to see Gregory relaxed again in his high-backed leather office chair. 'I'm not sure your accounts will be the right fit for our firm.'

Liz felt like saying something snappy but decided she needed to find Robert, now. Something very wrong was going on with *Guild and Glover*. She opened the door, closed it gently to make sure Gregory didn't think he'd rattled her and walked with her shoulders back, head high as she glided over the polished grey tiled floor heading straight for Jack's office.

44

Liz retrieved her phone, requesting a taxi on her phone app as her phone rang. She looked at the call display to confirm if the call was for her, *Fox Investigations* or *Foxy Escort*. Max's name flashed up.

'Hey Max. I'm just on my way back to the station to see Jack.'

'Can you go home instead? I've left Heather and Taiwo at your place because I need to take my gun in to Penny at the forensic lab.'

'Why?'

'I just need to be there before five today, so you better take over the baby-sitting.'

'Damn.' There was a moment of silence. 'Okay.' She hung up as the taxi pulled up outside, the smoky glass frontage of the building reflecting the streetscape back at her as she got in the back seat.

'Sorry, change of destination.' The taxi driver didn't seem bothered when Liz sent him to her apartment on North Terrace instead of the Major Crimes office on Angas Street, they were both only minutes away from North Adelaide.

The taxi pulled up in the valet area outside her apartment building a few minutes later. She paid the driver, including a small tip and slammed the door.

'Ms Jeffreys.' Bennie met her outside the entrance looking frazzled.

'What is it Bennie?'

'Your guests, the two girls. Max, your partner, not that type of partner...' Liz put a hand on his arm.

'Slow down Bennie. I know Max left, what about my guests?'

'They left, about five minutes ago.'

'Left, on foot?'

'No, a taxi collected them.'

'Damn.' She looked at the doorman's pained face. 'It's not your fault Bennie. You couldn't keep them here.'

She pulled her mobile out of her jacket pocket and dialled Jack's number. 'We have a problem.'

'What's up?'

'Heather and Taiwo skipped out in the ten minutes between Max leaving and me arriving home.'

'Shit!'

'Don't panic yet. I'll see if Scott can track them down.'

'Okay, I'll finish up here and meet you at your place.'

'I'll let Max know. Heather is definitely a handful. Why on earth would she leave?'

'Maybe Scott can tell you.'

'Good point. See you soon.' Liz hung up, looked at her watch to make sure Scott would be out of bed and called. It was nearly five, he'd have to be up by now.

The call went to message bank and Liz left an urgent message as she entered the foyer and pressed the call button on the elevator.

Her phone rang as she stepped inside and pressed the top floor. 'Scott. Sorry to bother you. It's urgent or I wouldn't.'

'All good. My phone was still on silent. Missed you by half a sec. What's up?'

'Heather, you were tracing who was trying to track her.' He mumbled affirmative. 'Can you see who texted her last and what the text was?'

'Technically yes, morally no.'

'I will make sure no one presses charges.'

'You might have the cops wrapped around your finger, but Heather is another story. That woman can be down-right dangerous.'

'I didn't realise you knew her that well.'

'Long story. Is it really *that* urgent?'

'Could be life or death Scott.'

'Oh, now that's dramatic. No pressure.' Scott's fingers were already typing. Liz could hear them in the background as she opened her apartment door hoping Heather left some sort of message and they were just heading out for a movie or something, but she knew she was clutching at straws.

Heather seemed to be focussed on solving the unsolved. Fixated even. The young woman reminded her too much of herself.

'Okay. She's turned her phone off so I can't track her now, but....'

'What is it?'

'The last message she got is a bit cryptic.'

'Text it to me Scott.'

'Will do.'

'Can you trace the call?'

'No can do. Ask your cop friends. You'll need to get a hold of the telecommunications companies to triangulate the signal.'

'But you can hack Heather's number?'

'One isn't likely to end in a federal court case, the other could.'

'Okay, sorry I asked. Thanks for the help.'

'You're welcome.'

Scott hung up and Liz stared at her phone a moment before putting her bag on the kitchen counter and drawing her laptop closer, opening the lid and tapping the keys to bring up the screen.

A text from Scott arrived a few seconds later. *Kabo will be glad to see you.*

45

Liz opened the door to Jack. 'I came as quick as I could. Have you heard from Scott?'

'Only that he can't track Heather because her phone is off and he can't triangulate the incoming text because it's against the law. He said that's going to have to be up to your team.'

'Shit! We can't get a warrant for that unless she's officially missing and less than an hour won't cut it with a judge.'

'The law sucks you know.' Jack nodded and Liz could see he was feeling powerless.

'Bridges ran our arson victim Montgomery through the database earlier and found he's got union ties. Been charged with aggravated assault a few years back. His drinking buddies are on the radar too. Jenny and Bridges were doing a late call on both.'

'Is that good or bad news?'

'Good in one way. There were three men in the van that tried to grab Heather. A driver, Montgomery who took a bullet from Max, ballistics still pending and another guy in the back trying to close the door.'

'So you think his union buddies might be the accomplices?'

'It's a start.'

'Yes, but Heather and Taiwo have gone to see Taiwo's brother Kabo and something about the text message just feels ominous to me.' Liz showed Jack the message Scott had forwarded to her.

'*Third person.*'

'Exactly. I don't think Kabo sent that message Jack.'

'I agree.'

'Jack, Bennie said they went by taxi. Can we call the taxi company and ask where the pick-up dropped them off?'

'We can, but probably not until the morning when their administration staff are in. Jenny and Bridges will be here after they've checked on the two union buddies. Anderson is already on his way. Maybe he can find out more through the federal investigation that's surrounding Kruger and Baxter's construction company.'

'Maybe.'

'I'll see if Jenny can get anything out of the taxi company. She's usually pretty good at sweet talking over the phone. Otherwise we'll go down tomorrow morning first thing.'

'Okay, but I'm not sure waiting to find Heather and Taiwo is a good idea. If someone is using Taiwo's brother to lure them out of hiding, it could be dangerous for them both.'

'What could Heather know that they want so much?'

'Maybe it's what Taiwo knows or maybe they just want to make sure neither of them knows enough. Either way, these guys don't seem to like to leave live witnesses around for long.'

'You're right. We'll get onto the taxi as soon as the team are all here.'

'I also met Gregory today.'

'And?'

'And Robert is apparently off *sick*.' Liz used air quotes on the word. 'Any chance you can get a uniformed unit to call around and check on him?'

'Your Foxy nose twitching?' Jack moved toward Liz, taking her in his arms and gently kissing her nose. She wanted to kiss him back, but her stomach was tossing around like she was on a Royal Adelaide show ride.

'It is. Can you send a unit? It was something Gregory said that made me think Robert might be in trouble.'

'I'll call now.' Jack let Liz go and reached for his flip phone.

'Jack, there's something else.' Jack stopped, phone mid-air on the way to his ear, the ring tone loud enough to hear the police despatch pick up.

'Detective Cunningham, badge number two, five, four, two, one. I need a unit to head over to speak to someone, just to run a check on something relating to a homicide investigation. Yes, case number H two-four-two-nine-nine.'

'Thanks. Send them to the home address of Robert Glover and ask them to call my personal mobile when they get on scene.'

'No, sorry I don't have the address.' He looked at Liz who shrugged. She'd never met with Robert anywhere but a private suite in a Hindley Street apartment building. Likely his city apartment, but she'd never asked.'

'Can you run his driver's licence records?' Jack waited while the despatcher checked. 'Aged late fifties, early sixties. He'll likely live within the Adelaide Metro area.' A few more seconds passed. 'Yes, that would be him. Thanks. I appreciate it. No, just a precaution. He's a witness in our investigation and he's not been reachable all day.'

Jack hung up and turned to Liz. 'What were you going to say before?'

'Gregory pretty much threatened me to back off.'

'Back off what? What did you ask him?'

'I asked him about his visits to Oasis Resort and his relationship with the De Beers.'

'What did he say to that?'

'He told me that *Guild and Glover* wouldn't be taking on my accounts.'

'Really. Doubt he has that authority.' Jack smirked.

'Me neither, which is why I thought Richard might be in trouble, but the big thing I did notice while I was in his office is that he looks a lot like the guy in the game hunting photo I showed you. Older, but I think it's him.'

'Are you sure?'

'Pretty sure and judging by his reaction to my question, I'd stake my life on it.'

'I'd prefer it if you didn't.

46

Jack leant in to kiss her lips softly, she didn't resist. Heather and Taiwo's disappearance niggled at the back of her mind, but the smell of Jack's fading aftershave and the scent that she'd come to know as him, drew her focus away from her worries.

His lips touched lightly, moving to her earlobe which sent tingles to her toes. As she wrapped her arms around his neck, he pulled her to him, the kiss becoming more desperate. She mirrored his anxiousness, pulling his jacket off and throwing it on the kitchen counter. It landed, just before the door buzzer sounded.

'That was quick.' Jack's voice was husky.

'Too quick.' Liz let her arms drop away, reaching for the security tablet as Jack carefully laid his jacket over the back of a white leather barstool.

The buzzer sounded again, as Liz spotted Max's face pressed up against the fisheye lens. Pressing the *open* button, she allowed the door to activate automatically.

'I only left ten minutes before you.' He walked into the apartment and headed straight for Liz's fridge. She had no doubt about what he was fishing for in there. Retrieving a beer, he held one up to see if Jack was as keen as he was. Jack nodded the affirmative and Max withdrew two Coopers Ale stubbies, screwing the top off the first and sculling half of it before taking the few steps and sliding the other down the shiny stone bar to Jack.

Jack didn't hesitate. He too unscrewed the top and took a long, slow gulp before putting it down and heading to the kitchen to reach for a wine glass for Liz.

The buzzer sounded again, this time the hallway was full of familiar faces and Liz opened the door to greet Anderson, Bridges and Jenny.

'You two were quick.' Jack called, the bottle of wine still in hand.

'It wasn't hard. The two guys we were looking for were off the grid.' Jenny looked like she'd run, not driven around town looking for Montgomery's union buddies while Bridges stood to the side, his hands in his pockets just watching the close-knit group he was yet to fully become a part of.

'What does that mean?' Jack brought the wine glass over to Liz and returned for another, knowing Hemi wasn't keen on beer. 'Wine mate?' The Kiwi nodded.

'Thanks bro. I just got chewed out by my CO and it wasn't pretty.'

'Is that because of our investigation?' Jack filled the glass and passed it to Hemi who had joined him in the kitchen.

'Yes and no. I'm not technically in the loop, but to help you guys out and to satisfy my own curiosity, I asked a mate of mine who's been involved in the recent investigation. He was also on board in the first investigation into the De Beers back in '09.'

'What did you find out?' Max moved to Liz's fridge and retrieved three beers.

'Hey, go easy Max, I've only got a few in there and you might need to drive somewhere.'

Max peered into the fridge and looked back over his shoulder. 'You had a full carton in here last week.' He stared at his ex-partner accusingly but wisely decided to let the matter drop when Liz gave him the evil eye.

'I found out that Marilyn's parents didn't just never leave Australia, but their credit cards and bank accounts haven't been touched either.'

'That sounds like they've been murdered too then.' Liz ushered everyone to her large dining table. The glass table and leather chairs offered seating for eight while her counter stools topped out at four.

'Not necessarily.' Jack was first to take a seat in the high-back chair, letting out a sigh that everyone heard.

'Sounds pretty ominous to me.' Jenny agreed with Liz and took a seat, nodding and pursing her lips to say she agreed with Jack's sigh. 'These are comfier than they look.'

'They could have changed identities,' Max added.

'Maybe witness protection?' Bridges joined the conversation for the first time.

'That was my first assumption.' Anderson sat down next to Jenny, his large bulky frame somehow seemed in proportion to the chair. 'But then we wouldn't offer witness protection to South African citizens and there was no case where I could find that they bore witness that would warrant relocation like that.'

'So we are back to dead or false identity,' Max concluded.

'Actually, can we hold this thought for now? Jack, we need to track that taxi.' Liz tried to bring the large group of inquisitive investigators back on track.

'You should head up my squad room meetings,' he grinned. 'Liz is right. Taiwo and Heather have headed to meet Kabo, Taiwo's brother, only both Liz and I don't think Kabo organised the meeting. Which can only mean something bad could be around the corner. Jenny, can you call the taxi company and find out who did a pickup just before five this afternoon outside Liz's building?'

Jenny grabbed her phone from her pocket and began to make a call.

'So you got nowhere with Montgomery's mates?'

Bridges looked up from studying his beer, a surprised look on his face when he realised he needed to give Jack an update. 'Like Williams said. Neither were home, neither have been home for a few days.'

'So have they legged it or are we going to find them dead too?' Jack asked the question generally, not really expecting an answer.

'I don't think they'd even know Montgomery is dead yet. Not if they've been running errands for whoever ordered Heather's break-in and kidnapping.'

'Could be right Bridges. And we are dealing with someone far cleverer than Montgomery's crew of union heavies. The cameras near Heather's home were wiped clean and Heather didn't think there was any reason Marshall would have done it.'

'So whoever is trying to silence Taiwo and Heather, has computer experts who can hack the servers of the security company that run the street cams.' Liz drummed her fingers on the glass table as she shared her thoughts.

'We have a construction company with links to the De Beers. We have an accounting manager and firm linked to the De Beers and we have three jewellers who Marilyn was investigating linked to the De Beers with funds being transferred.' Jack summarised.

'I also found out that Kruger is married, but I haven't been able to pull his marriage certificate from South Africa yet.'

'How did you find that out?' Jack sat back, taking another sip of his beer.

'It's in the surveillance case file.' Anderson's face took on a look of a mischievous child.

'You managed to sneak a peek?' Liz tried to hide her excitement.

'Yeah, that was what I got grilled for before I came here.'
'Why?'

'Because there are lots of people working on this from South Africa, the US and Australia.'

'So it's got to be blood diamonds. Illegal game hunting wouldn't bring down forces from three countries.' Jack got up to grab another beer as Jenny got off the phone.

'I've got an address.'

'That was easy.' Jack seemed surprised.

'I know people,' Jenny grinned. 'The driver dropped off the pick-up at forty-nine Lipson Street.'

'Isn't that…' Jack looked to Max for confirmation.

'It is.' Jenny and Max spoke in unison.

'Anderson. Is there anything in that file about this location?'

Hemi screwed up his face a moment, knowing where this was going and not liking it one bit. 'Not that I saw but I didn't read the whole file.'

'Well if the AFP don't want to share information with us, and we accidentally stumble into their investigation chasing down a possible kidnapping, then there won't be anything they can do.'

Jack's phone rang and he moved away from the table to answer it. Hemi was left with no rebuttal. Instead, he looked at Jenny, his eyes begging her not to step into a federal investigation, but he said nothing.

'That was the uniformed unit we sent to Robert Glover's home.' Liz stood up as she watched Jack bouncing on the balls of his feet, ready to run a sprint. 'They said the place had been turned over and no one was home.'

'Did you get anything on the van from the warehouse Bridges?' Max turned to the latest recruit to the team.

'It was registered to the warehouse location.'

'What was the company name on the building?'

'I don't remember?'

'Then call into the office now mate. I'm sure the night duty crew won't mind.' Jack didn't hide his frustration. It was obvious he thought Bridges should have been more thorough following up the leads on registration as asked. 'If Glover's place has been turned over, they might have worked out he was helping Liz with the jeweller's information.'

'We did say Kruger looked to be cleaning house,' Liz added as Jack grabbed his jacket and headed toward the door.

'You think he's going to run?' Anderson was on his feet now. 'I should probably tip off the task force.'

'Not yet. We need to make sure we get Heather and Taiwo and her brother if he's there too.'

'Jack, we could be too late. The girls have been there since five-thirty.' Liz felt her stomach doing summersaults.

'Let's hope we aren't. We'll head out there now and see if we can get a look inside.' Jack turned to Anderson. 'I don't suppose we can borrow Kent and his drone again?'

'If push comes to shove, call me but I'm not going over the task force's head unless I have to, and unless you *know* Kruger is in that warehouse, it's not federal, you said so yourself.' Hemi grinned and Jenny squeezed his arm, mouthing 'thank you'.

'When you're done Bridges, do a drive by Heather's house, make sure they haven't picked up another taxi and headed home. Save us running around like chooks with our heads cut off.' Max opened the front door and held it for the rest of the team to file out.

'Who made you boss?' Bridges grumbled, but Jack nodded and he shrugged to say he'd do it, reluctantly.

47

Jack opened the passenger's side door for Liz and rushed around the bonnet to the driver's side. Jenny rode with Max in case they needed to head in different directions.

Jack slid in behind the wheel and started the car, looking to Liz as though he was unsure about dragging her out into possible danger. She placed her hand on his arm and smiled. 'It's what we do.' Jack shook his head and returned the gesture.

'It's what *you* usually do. Charge head first into danger.'

'We need to get Heather and Taiwo to safety.'

'Yes, but not at the expense of everyone else involved. They went off without telling anyone.'

'I think Heather doesn't really trust the police.'

'I agree. But I thought she trusted us.' Jack drove the car away from the curb, checking his rear-view mirror to make sure Max was following behind.

'Don't take it personally Jack. I get her, in a bizarre kind of way I understand her mistrust.'

Jack waited, unsure if he should ask Liz to elaborate. She knew if she'd told him she'd explain her story, but was now really the right time? Probably not, but his eyes were asking the question anyway.

'My mum's boyfriend raped me, when I was fifteen.' The silence felt heavy and Liz looked at her hands, trying to decide if she needed or wanted to share her past. 'I didn't want to tell my mum, because it would have sent her over the edge.'

'I'm sorry Liz. I wish castration was a real sentence option.' Jack focussed on the darkening road as dusk approached and the streetlights twinkled into existence.

In another situation, the scene might have been romantic, but Liz's heart was racing for all the wrong reasons. How would Jack feel about more sordid stories from her past?

'It was the eighties and the local police station told me to tell my mum. They said I didn't have any proof, so there was nothing they could do. It would be his word against mine and if my mum wouldn't vouch for me, then they couldn't do anything.'

'They didn't question him?' Liz shook her head, her focus back in her hands which she knew were fidgeting in her lap.

'I looked older than fifteen. I got the impression they thought I'd led Les on, but when I refused to tell my mum, they said they couldn't do anything.' She bit her lip, almost drawing blood as the memory flooded back with pain and fear.

'That's horrible. I'm sorry you had to go through that.' He reached out, drawing Liz's hand out from her lap and squeezing it.

'Me too, but I wouldn't be here if not for good old Les.'

Jack's phone rang and he pressed the historic Blue Ant hands-free unit on the back of his sun visor.

'I can't believe you still have one of those. It must be an antique by now.' Liz smiled as Bridges' voice came over the car stereo system louder than Jack intended. He spun the volume button down a little, grinning sheepishly.

'Bridges. What you got?'

'Overtime.'

'Yes mate. I'll log the hours for you.'

The owners of the warehouse and thereby our black van is a company named *The Wright Family Trust.*'

'That name rings a bell.' Liz pulled her mobile from her backpack and started searching the internet while Bridges carried on.

'You heading to Heather's now?'

'I'll grab something to eat, then I'll head past and do a drive-by, see if there are any lights on.'

'Thanks mate. See you tomorrow.'

'See ya.'

Jack pressed the *off* button on the hands-free unit and closed his sun visor, taking a peek to see what Liz was studying on her phone as he pulled down the street heading for the warehouse in Port Adelaide.

The old dockside area had loads of old warehouses from historical red bricked three-storey buildings to galvanised iron sheds that you could park a cruise-liner in, but many had been converted to residential living. That wasn't the case in Lipson Street, where timber merchants and import-export companies still housed their merchandise.

Liz looked over at Jack as the car stopped, her mobile held up for him to see. She'd done a quick search to see if the trust Bridges had mentioned had any registered trading names owned by the company and one was a standout.

Jack's eyebrows lifted as he read *Elegant and Elite* were one of four trading names linked to the company. Another was Baxter's construction company.

'As Jenny would say, curiouser and curiouser.'

'I think Alice in Wonderland took that line first.'

Jack opened the door and got out as Liz did the same on the other side. Jenny and Max parked behind them, a short distance down the road from the warehouse Max had been surveying.

'It looks deserted.' Liz said what everyone was thinking. No lights shone inside and the parking area outside was empty.

'If only Max hadn't been scared off by the goonies,' Jenny teased and Max took the bait.

'You didn't see the two guys haul me out of my car like a sack of potatoes.'

'Turns out the company that own this warehouse also trade as *Elegant and Elite*, and *Baxter Construction and Engineering*.'

'That can't be a coincidence. I should let Hemi know.'

'I think the Feds likely already know there's a link. What annoys me is they know we're investigating three murders, one a decade old and they've done their best to lock us out of the investigation.' Jack moved down the street toward the mesh fence, peering through the darkened parking lot to the warehouse beyond.

'No one is home mate. What next?'

'Let's hope that Heather and Taiwo are tucked up in bed at Heather's place, because if they aren't, I'm all out of ideas.' Jack looked as crestfallen as everyone felt, but he perked himself back up.

'Bridges said he was grabbing food before going home past Heathers. Let's head back to Liz's and hope for the best, but at least we'll all be together if we need to kick the search up a notch.'

'Good idea.' Liz fought the urge to grab Jack's hand and squeeze it to reassure him they'd find both the women they were looking for.

Jenny's phone buzzed on silent in her pocket. She retrieved it, and retreated from the group when she saw who the caller was. Liz smiled knowingly as both men rolled their eyes, barely visible in the dim street lighting.

'That was Hemi, ah Anderson.'

'It's all good Jenny, we're off the clock.'

'I thought Bridges was getting overtime.' Liz chuckled.

'That would be right. Lull the newbie into a false sense of security,' Max teased.

'Hemi said that the details about Kruger's marriage just came back and it ties all the strings together.' Jenny let the tension build a moment and Liz wondered if now was the time for theatrics, but the younger detective seemed to be having fun.

'Come on Jenny,' Jack finally pushed.

'Kruger is Tash De Beer's husband.'

'For fuck's sake. That ties *Elegant and Elite*, *Baxter Construction and Engineering*, someone inside *Guild and Glover* and the De Beer family and or *Oasis Game Reserve* into one tight little bundle. Max looked from Jack to Jenny, then his eyes finally rested on Liz, a satisfied grin tugged at the corners of his mouth.

'Yep, but it's all circumstantial Max.' Jack brought the skyrocket crashing down and Max's face followed the trajectory.

The idea hit Liz like a tidal wave. 'Kabo, Taiwo's brother. He must know what's been going on. He came with Taiwo, or followed her at least to help Heather on Marilyn's case. They didn't come to the police because the police aren't exactly beyond reproach where they come from.'

Jack picked up the idea running around Liz's brain. 'But Kruger, Tash's husband found out that Kabo was here, grabbed him, didn't know how much he'd told Heather or Taiwo and needed to use him as bait to clean up the whole mess.'

'Exactly. We need to find Heather. If Kruger has her and Taiwo, it's only a matter of time before he's sure he's cleaned house thoroughly enough to kill them both, and Kabo.' Liz was moving back to Jack's old BMW; Max and Jenny headed toward Max's Mazda, just as Jack's phone rang.

All four stopped outside the vehicles, hands hovering over door handles.

'Bridges. What's up?'

Liz's stomach was in her throat.

'I forgot to tell you.' Jack put the phone on speaker as Jenny and Max moved closer.

'What did you forget?'

'Baxter's older licence photos came back. According to the most recent photo, he's changed eye colour and aged only five years.'

'Did you run the new photo past Anderson?'

'No, I've got the night crew running it through state mug shots.'

'Call them now and ask them to send a copy to me. I'll see what Anderson can find out.' Jack looked at Max for confirmation that he thought it was the right thing to do. Max nodded he was on the same page.

'I'm five minutes from checking up on Heather's place at Saint Peters and then I'm off the clock.'

'The clock's still running Bridges. If Heather and Taiwo aren't there, we are going to have to find them, tonight.'

Bridges sigh was audible. 'Really!'

'Really. The company who owns the warehouse, also owns one of the jewellery firms Marilyn was concerned about, and Baxter's Construction.'

'Shit.'

'Exactly. Call me in five.' Jack hung up and all four eager investigators jumped into their vehicles and took off, wheels squealing toward Heather's house, with fingers and toes crossed that the women were both sitting around watching television with their feet up, but deep down, Liz knew that wasn't likely the case.

48

Jack's phone pinged with a texted photo as they drove down the Port River Expressway, heading to Saint Peters. He handed the phone to Liz, assuming it was the photo he'd been expecting.

'Can you text that on to Anderson?'

Liz nodded, grabbed the phone and opened it. The small flip phone made the photo difficult to see clearly and with no way of zooming in, Liz couldn't be sure, but the man in the licence looked a lot like one of the men in the photo with Gregory.

She sent the text on to Hemi with an explanation, hoping he'd be by his phone since Jenny was out with them. The thumbs up logo appeared and Liz couldn't help but think of Max who seemed to communicate solely with emojis these days.

'He's checking, but I think I've seen this guy in that game hunting photo we saw of a younger Gregory at the Oasis Reserve. Did you ever meet Marilyn's parents?'

'Nope.'

'Ever see a photo?'

'No, she didn't talk about them at all. All she said when we started dating was that she left under difficult circumstances and as far as she was concerned, she didn't have a family.'

'That's a tough stance.' Liz thought of her own mother and thirty years of absence. In that moment, she knew that whatever reason Marilyn had had for leaving her family in her past, it was a bloody good one.

'If they were the type of people who could kill their own daughter, then she had a damn good reason for never wanting to have anything to do with them after she left.' Jack's face looked hard in the light of oncoming vehicles. He was angry, frustrated, sad and Liz couldn't blame him.

Jack's phone buzzed in Liz's hand, she flipped it open and answered as soon as she confirmed who the caller was. 'Liz here Hemi. I've got you on speaker. What have you got?

'That photo matches the federal file on De Beer, missing for ten years.'

'Thanks Hemi.' She was just about to flip the phone closed.

'I've put my team on standby, you let me know if you need them Jack.'

Jack leant over so Hemi wouldn't miss his answer. 'I will, thanks mate.' He nodded to Liz to end the call.

Jack turned left off South Road onto Regency Road as his phone rang again. Liz opened it and put the call on speaker allowing Jack to answer.

'Go ahead Bridges.'

'I've just pulled up outside Heather's place. The lights are on and I was just about to head home and leave the place for you to chase up, but something isn't right about this picture Cunningham.'

'What is it?' Liz rolled her eyes and waved her hand like she was directing traffic, trying to coax an answer out of Bridges who obviously couldn't see her.

'There are two cars in the driveway. I wasn't sure what car she drives, but then I saw a black van, the rego matches the one Max saw entering the warehouse.'

'We are only two minutes out Bridges. Stay out of sight but let us know if anything happens.'

'Will do.' The phone went dead and Liz flipped it closed, her eyes scanning Jack's face as the street lights illuminated him in three second intervals.

'What now? Do we call Hemi's team in?'

'My gut tells me we don't have time. If Heather had something Kruger wanted hidden in her house, the guy will have it very soon and all three of his hostages will be dead before Anderson's task force team arrives.'

'You can't go in with handguns Jack. You, Jenny, Max and Bridges aren't trained for hostage situations.'

'I know, but we don't have a choice!'

Liz bit her lip, a plan forming in her mind as Jack's car pulled over down the street from Heather's house.

'You're not going to like this Detective.' Jack looked over at her, his hand on the door ready to jump out, but he stopped at her tone and expression.

'I know I'm not when you call me Detective. Nothing good ever happens when you do.'

Liz grinned. 'I wouldn't say that. You remember the time...'

'Okay, you win. What are you thinking?'

'I'm thinking we better wait until Max and Jenny get here and Bridges joins us. I only want to fight about this once.' Liz opened the door and pushed it closed quietly, Jack did the same on the driver's side as Max's car pulled up behind them.

49

Jack watched the curtains flicker on the front living room window of Heather's colonial cottage as he mulled over Liz's plan. It was a good one and in any other circumstance he would have been only too pleased to run with it, but Liz's life was on the line again and he wasn't about to let anything happen to her.

'We should call Hemi.' Jenny looked from face to face and Max shook his head.

'Jack's right, it could be too late. We can't take that chance. There is a least one, if not three hostages in there.' Max pointed to the cottage that looked frightening in the moonlight, a lonely street lamp shining dimly down the driveway.

A dull light shone through the lounge-room window, while a beam of pale light shone through the glass entrance door, creating an eerie glow from within.

'Max, you and Bridges go down the driveway, to the rear of the house.' Jack drew a quick outline of the interior layout from memory. Jenny looked over his shoulder, nodded that he had it accurate as far as her memory recalled.

'To cover out butts, we'll call Anderson, but they won't get here in time. Since this case is part ours, part federal and we know we likely have two South African citizens inside, we should have him on scene to help clean up.'

'Hopefully there isn't much left to clean up. I don't need any more black marks on my record Cunningham.' Jack stared at Bridges, but all thought of opening that comment up to questions slipped away as Liz patted him on the shoulder.

'We're running out of time and you're stalling. I know you are. Call Anderson now, I'm going in.' Liz moved toward the stone pathway that led to the centrally located porch and entrance, but Jack moved forward before she crossed the road, pulling her into the shadow of a tall Jacaranda tree, the purple petals of the flowers floated down in the light spring breeze and in any other situation, the scene would have been beautiful, but right now Jack's adrenalin was firing.

'Be careful.' He pushed Liz further into the shadows, brushing his lips against hers. 'I've gotten very used to having you around.'

'The feeling is mutual.' The sound of raised voices from inside Heather's home reached them. Liz pushed away from the tree, gently avoiding a protective embrace from Jack. 'I need to get in there.'

'Give us thirty seconds to get into position.' Jack rushed back the few metres to where Bridges' car was parked, Max, Bridges and Jenny all tucked down behind it.

Liz nodded and moved across the quiet suburban street, avoiding the streetlight that illuminated the driveway.

Jack watched her move away, his heart racing, his mind desperately trying to catch up.

****

Liz jumped at the sound of something smashing beyond the dining room window as she moved up the two steps to Heather's porch. To stop her hands from shaking, she put them into her pants pockets as she took three, long, slow breaths.

Another sound, this time a thud. *Oh God, get your shit together Liz.* She'd never walked right into a hostile situation like this before. Sure, she'd been kidnapped and nearly killed but this was different. This time she knew she was up against a killer and her job in all of this was to play interference—be the distraction while Jack and his team hopefully got into position.

She pulled her right hand from her pocket, balled a fist and bashed on the front door. Silence greeted her. An eerie lack of noise from the earlier thuds and crashes was even more frightening. *Had Kruger killed them already? Was she too late?*

'Heather. It's Mrs Grant, from number nine. I heard about your dog and just wanted to call by.'

There was no answer as Liz saw Bridges and Max disappear down the left-hand side of the building to the garage, past the outside of the black van and another car they'd not bothered to check registration on.

She knocked again. 'Heather, I know you are home. I know it must be hard, losing your dog after everything you've been through. I just thought you might need a friend.' Liz called through the wooden door, the two colonial style glass panels showed movement beyond. Liz pulled back, her heart climbing into her throat, higher and higher with every thundering beat.

The dining room window curtain flickered. Liz caught sight of Heather's black goth fingernails, hoping the young woman would play along, knowing help wasn't far away.

A few seconds passed, before Heather appeared at the door, opening it a crack, someone obviously putting her under duress.

'Mrs Grant. Thanks for thinking of me, but I'm fine.' Heather's voice quavered and she winced, as thought someone might be holding a knife or gun at her side. Liz felt powerless, for the first time in her life since she'd left her lonely street-kid days behind. She felt totally inadequate for the challenge.

'I can come in. Even if it's for a second.' Liz didn't wait for an answer. She shoved at the door with her full weight, hoping against hope that the slide lock wasn't in place. There would be no way she could shoulder the heavy door open if it were, but there was also no way she was going to let that door close, locking Heather away with whoever was threatening her.

The door flew open as she threw what little weight she had into it, Heather stumbled back, a tall, lean man fell back into the dining area behind the door. Liz felt like she was floating above her body as the guy lost his footing and hit the floor, obviously not expecting an older neighbour of Heather's to shove the door open, let alone with a full hip and shoulder.

A feral growl made Liz cringe as the man tried to get to his feet. Heather jumped forward and Liz realised it was her howling as she laid a Doc Martin into the side of her assailant.

'What the fuck!' The face of the man who walked out of the kitchen area, into the dining room where Heather was laying into the guy on the floor was only too familiar to Liz.

He looked from his henchman on the floor, to Heather, his eyes finally resting on Liz. Even in the dim lighting, they clearly recognised each other.

'Mr Gregory. We meet again.'

'Stop it!' He pulled a gun up from his side, aiming it central mass on Heather's chest. The young goth orphan wasn't holding back, the guy on the ground now fully unconscious. Liz moved forward, placing her hand on Heather's arm and squeezing firmly.

'You have to stop.' Her tone was soft. 'You'll kill him and he'll kill you.' Liz nodded toward Gregory, standing, waving his gun frantically. Liz wasn't sure the guy had the guts to use it, but she wasn't about to test her theory, not when they were both sitting ducks.

The sound of voices, shouting, crashing, thudding reached Liz, as Heather finally saw Gregory looming over them.

'Armed Police! Put your weapons down!' Liz struggled to recognise the voice amongst all the noise and commotion.

Gregory grabbed her arm, pushed her toward Heather and the front door. This wasn't part of the plan. Where was Jack? Liz felt sick, as the gun waved before her eyes and she dragged Heather out onto the porch, away from everyone she knew could protect her.

50

Max saw Kruger first. The guy stood over an African man, his head covered in bruises, the left eye swollen shut like a prize boxer.

The other guy looked like hired muscle, short, wide, steroid-induced neck muscles that looked as though he'd spent too many hours pumping iron in the gym or maybe behind bars.

'Hands in the air.' Kruger obliged, a smarmy grin crossing his lips like he was going to walk away scot-free any second.

The other guy barged, like a bull, full pelt toward Max, who sidestepped hoping Jenny wasn't right behind him. Fortunately, Bridges had entered after him and Max heard the thump before the thud of the man's body hit the hardwood timber floor.

Max moved forward, grabbed the gun out of Kruger's shoulder holster, and passed it back to Jenny being careful not disturb any prints.

The sound of movement at the front of the house made him fly past Kruger, nodding for Bridges to do the honours since he didn't carry cuffs.

He saw Taiwo, huddled in the corner, tears running down her face, her eyes staring into space like she'd seen a ghost. She wasn't in any immediate danger. Where was Heather? He needed to find Heather. The girl had grown on him, he now knew he had a soft spot for her. If anything happened to her, he'd never forgive himself.

The sound of voices in the front room caught his attention. He moved into the dimly lit dining area in time to see a tall, lean man push Heather and Liz out the front door.

****

Jack moved forward as he saw Liz force her way inside. That wasn't part of the deal, but Liz was always going off script. He should have known and been prepared for her to do something stupid. She was only supposed to distract everyone in the house, not push her way inside. That was Jack's job.

He was three steps from the landing when Liz's terrified face appeared in the doorway, Heather a step behind. Gregory was armed, looking just as frightened as Liz.

An armed man with adrenalin rushing through his head, fear following close behind was never a good combination. The sound of sirens in the distance told Jack his armed response unit was on the way, but Liz and Heather might not have five seconds, let alone five minutes.

Jack's gun was already tracking Gregory as Liz took the first step down from the porch.

'Police!' Jack took aim, his left leg slightly further forward than his right, braced and ready to fire. 'Put down your weapon! Hands in the air!'

Gregory tried to grab Heather, but she wasn't a tiny, timid woman on any normal day and Jack could see she was in a fighting mood. She pushed him away, into Liz who was only a couple of metres away from him now. So close, but not close enough.

Gregory grabbed Liz around the neck and pushed the gun into the side of her head. Liz's eyes met his and for a second, he didn't know what to do. He trained on the shooting range, he was an excellent shot, but this was Liz's head right next to Gregory's and a head shot was all he had.

Gregory's eyes darted to the road as Anderson's truck pulled up, his team piling out like the perfectly well trained federal officers they were. Jack took a deep breath. This wasn't any ordinary hostage situation, this was Liz.

Heather screamed from the side of the porch. 'Let her go you bastard!' and for a second Jack thought the highly-strung goth girl was going to leap at Gregory, but Max appeared by her side, his gun trained on Gregory's back. He wrapped his arm tightly around Heather.

Max's sheer bulk held her in place, her arms trapped at her side, up against his ex-partner's broad chest.

'Put the gun down Gregory.' Max's tone was ominous, and Gregory took his eyes from Jack to look over his shoulder at the unexpected voice from behind him.

'Put it down now Gregory, before the federal team shoots your head off. They don't play nice in hostage situations. You have three seconds to comply!' Gregory's eyes darted back to Jack, his gun hand began to shake.

'Do what they say Gregory. They *will* kill you.' Liz spoke quietly. Jack could only just hear her. 'They did last time someone held me hostage. Every single man died with a high-powered bullet in their brain.' Liz's tone was scaring Jack, it had to have Gregory shitting himself.

The man pushed her away from him, dropping to his knees. He tossed the gun to the grass below the porch. Anderson's men rushed in, knocking him onto his face, his arms roughly pulled around behind his back and cuffs pulled tight around his wrists.

'Where's Kruger?' Anderson moved forward with two more of his team, automatic rifles raised, fully alert.

'Secure in the dining room.' Max pointed as Heather began to sob into his chest. 'It's okay now. Max is here.'

Liz turned to see Heather was alright before rushing into Jack's arms, burying her face into him.

'You have to stop doing this!' He knew there was no force in his words as he wrapped his left arm around her waist and kissed the top of her head, the scent of her hair helping to force his heart to slow down. She was safe. For now.

51

Anderson reappeared a few minutes later, pushing Kruger out the front door ahead of him, in cuffs. He handed the Saffa over to two of his team members and stopped on the porch to wait for Jenny and Bridges to catch up before meeting Jack at the bottom of the porch steps.

'You were cutting that fine bro.' His bright smile breaking up the darkness.

'It wasn't how we planned it mate, but we had to go in. We could hear Heather was running out of time.' He looked at Liz, still wrapped firmly in his arms. She laid her head on his chest.

'That's what I'll put in the report.' Jenny smiled at him before moving toward Liz, her finger shaking before her.

'What's going on here?' She looked into Liz's eyes, before grinning like a school kid. 'I knew you'd get your act together eventually.'

'They had to, the tension was killing us.' Max moved down the doorstep, Heather still tucked under his protective arm.

'Why did Kruger bring you here?' Liz ignored her friends, preferring to focus on the case. It was safer.

'I told him I had evidence, that if he killed us, like he was planning, would be found by the cops.'

'Smart.' Max nodded approval. 'Did you?'

'Did I what?'

'Have evidence?'

'Hell no, but I had to stall. I knew Liz and you'd be fuming once we snuck out so I was hoping you'd track us down.'

'You could have left more details. Like a note that said where you were going.' Max's fatherly tone was kicking back in now, the sympathy and empathy waning.

'That would have been too easy.' Heather was getting over the shock, her voice having that usual edge of defiance.

'Where you taking him?' Jack pointed to Kruger as the AFP team loaded him into a police wagon.

'He offered to roll over the moment we arrested him.' Anderson looked over his shoulder to make sure no one else could hear. 'But I saw the African woman and her brother inside. I'm hoping we don't need Kruger's testimony and we nail his arse as hard to the wall as the rest of the De Beer family.'

'Did he tell you where Robert Glover is?' Liz suddenly felt anxious over her missing accountant.

'He was bailed up in his panic room when we sent a team over there to investigate the break in.'

'Who sent you over?' Liz looked at Jack who shrugged like he didn't know what was going on, but she could see he did.'

'I wanted to make sure your old friend was okay.' She kissed his cheek, thankful he wasn't seeing her old clients as any threat now. 'You arrested De Beer senior yet?' Jack looked back at Anderson.

'The original AFP team have headed to Baxter's residence now. All ports and airports are covered. He won't get away.'

'Famous last words.' Jack's draped his arm protectively over Liz's shoulder. 'Did you find Marilyn's mother?'

'Not yet. The real Baxter didn't have a wife, she passed away over twenty years ago, so Mrs De Beer could be dead like Marilyn.' Liz watched Jack's face as Anderson spoke, but the cringe she expected on hearing Marilyn's name didn't appear.

'She's probably on some island in the Caribbean or somewhere else we can't get extradition from. Marilyn never spoke fondly of any of her family.'

'It seems the apple didn't fall far from the tree when it comes to Tash. She and her brother have been handling the Botswana end of this smuggling machine for over a decade.' Jack's eyebrows rose, questioning if Anderson had been holding back. The Kiwi smiled, knowingly. 'I just got briefed on the way here. Don't shoot the messenger.'

'They've known all along?'

'Not about Baxter being De Beer. The AFP have been on surveillance over the operation for months.'

'So, it *was* AFP goons that pulled me out of my car at the warehouse?' Max looked offended Anderson hadn't told the truth.

'It was, but they didn't tell me that either. These investigations are tightly segmented so we don't get leaks. Or if we do, the suspect pool is small. I hope you understand. I'd hate to lose my drinking buddy over AFP business.'

Max rubbed his chin as if seriously contemplating the idea. 'You drink wine. That's hardly a drinking buddy.' Max let the thought sink in. 'But I'll make an exception.' Everyone laughed, even Heather, but as the ambulance team brought Kabo out on a gurney, they all fell silent.

'He's pretty knocked about.' Heather moved toward Taiwo, who was wrapped in a thermal blanket with a paramedic helping her down the porch steps behind her brother.

'What were they trying to find out?' Jack moved forward, putting his hand up to stop the paramedic pushing the gurney toward the ambulance.

'They wanted to know everything he knew. Then they wanted to use him to draw Taiwo and me out so they could tidy up any loose ends.'

'What does Kabo know?' Anderson looked interested. This was the break he was hoping for.

'Everything. He's worked for the De Beers for years and what he didn't know, Taiwo did from her work in the diamond export company. It wasn't until Marilyn's remains were found that Taiwo and he flew out here, hoping to help uncover this mess.'

'You should have brought them to us straight away Heather. This could all have been avoided.' Jack studied Kabo's head injuries as he spoke.

'I tried.' She looked at Taiwo, who was still too shocked to speak. 'But they were too scared of the police—of anyone in authority. They saw me as independent. It wasn't until Liz and Max came on board and I spent time with them that I could even convince her to stay under your protection.'

'Look at this.' Jack waved Liz over. 'We'll only be a second.' He spoke to the paramedic who nodded. 'What does that look like to you?'

'It looks like an emblem.'

'Like a signet ring maybe?' Liz grinned as Jack pulled back with a smug look on his face.'

'It does. Who did the beating Heather?' Liz turned around as Jack waved the paramedics on to the ambulance.

'Kruger. Why?'

'Because, if I'm right, we don't just have this little ring on kidnapping, smuggling and attempted murder, we have them, or specifically Kruger on three counts of murder.'

Anderson looked at Jack, his face showing his obvious confusion.

'Doc told me that the last victim, Montgomery, had a distinctive wound pattern on his head that he should be able to analyse while cleaning the bones. I think the signet ring impressions on Kabo's head injuries will match that wound and if it does, it will also match Kruger's family crest signet ring. Marilyn had one. I didn't think of it until now.'

'That's bloody awesome.' Max almost whooped, but stopped himself. 'That fucker was really starting to piss me off. When I broke down the rear door, the smug look on his face told me he was planning a rollover. You have no idea how happy that news makes me.'

'But did he kill Declan?' Heather's hands were on her hips now, the indignant look had returned.

'I'm not sure the AFP or even the local police can take that case on for you. The RSPCA maybe?'

Liz chuckled under her breath. She knew Declan meant a lot to Heather, but the fact Max was keen to pursue RSPCA charges for animal cruelty on top of three counts of murder was amusing, even to her.

'Is it too late for beer?' Max asked the collective who groaned as they moved towards their vehicles, ready to go their separate ways. 'But what's next? Do we have another case?'

Liz waved at Max as Jack put his arm around her waist and pulled her close.

'Come on. Someone must want a beer.' Max begged.

'Well. It looks like my house is a crime scene. Again!'

'Excellent, my recliner misses you already.'

'Your place or mine.' Jack whispered in her ear and even though she was more fatigued than she'd felt since her last kidnapping, the idea of having Jack permanently in her bed gave her a renewed sense of energy.

'My place is closer.'

Review and Follow

I'd love to know what you thought of this fifth instalment in the *Foxy Mysteries Series*, so give me your feedback at your favourite retailer website.

I am loving writing this series, and I also enjoy keeping in touch with my readers. I have lots to share and I can often use a little help with cover ideas, advanced readers and even the occasional survey. Most of all, I want to have the chance to give you even more value with occasional giveaways or great deals from myself and other authors I know.

Join my readers club to find out more about my writing, my background, my author friends and of course, you'll be the first to know when I release more books.

Visit www.atime2write.com.au - just click on the top banner to join the club.

Books by Fiona Tarr

Foxy Mysteries

Book 1 – Death Beneath the Covers
Book 2 – Presumed Missing
Book 3 – Deadly Deceit
Book 4 – Twisted Vendetta
Book 5 – Dead Cold

Opal Field Murders

Book 1 – Her Buried Bones Coming late 2022
Book 2 – Her Broken Bones Coming late 2022

Covenant of Grace Series

Book 1 – Destiny of Kings
Book 2 – Seed of Hope
Book 3 – Legacy of Power
Book 4 – Heir of Vengeance
Prequel – The Ehud Dagger Novella

The Eternal Realm

Book 1 – The Jericho Prophecy
Book 2 – Delilah and the Dark God
Book 3 – Reign of Retribution

The Priestess Chronicles

Book 1 – Call of the Druids
Book 2 – Relic Seeker
Book 3 – Shiloh Rising